ADVENTURES IN MAKERSPACE

A 3-D PRINTING MISSION

WRITTEN BY
SHANNON MCCLINTOCK MILLER
AND
BLAKE HOENA

ILLUSTRATED BY
ALAN BROWN

STONE ARCH BOOKS
a capstone imprint

capstone®

www.mycapstone.com

A 3-D Printing Mission is published by Stone Arch Books,
a Capstone imprint
1710 Roe Crest Drive, North Mankato, Minnesota 56003
www.mycapstonepub.com

Library of Congress Cataloging-in-Publication Data is available on the Library of Congress website.

ISBN: 978-1-4965-7745-0 (hardcover)
ISBN: 978-1-4965-7749-8 (paperback)
ISBN: 978-1-4965-7753-5 (eBook PDF)

Book design and art direction: Mighty Media
Editorial direction: Kellie M. Hultgren
Music direction: Elizabeth Draper
Music written and produced by Mark Mallman

Printed and bound in the United States of America.
PA017

CONTENTS

Download the Capstone 4D app!

- Ask an adult to download the Capstone 4D app.
- Scan the cover and stars inside the book for additional content.

When you scan a spread, you'll find fun extra stuff to go with this book! You can also find these things on the web at www.capstone4D.com using the password: 3dpr.77450

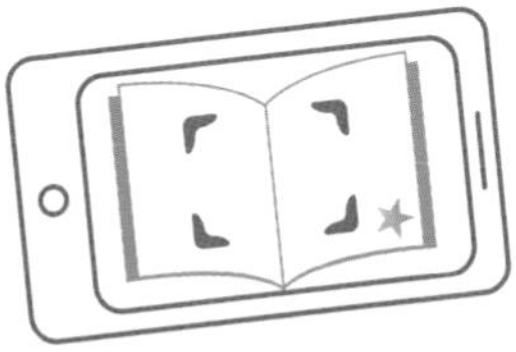

MEET THE SPECIALIST

ABILITIES:
speed reader, tech titan,
foreign language master,
traveler through literature
and history

MS. GILLIAN
TEACHER-LIBRARIAN

MEET THE STUDENTS

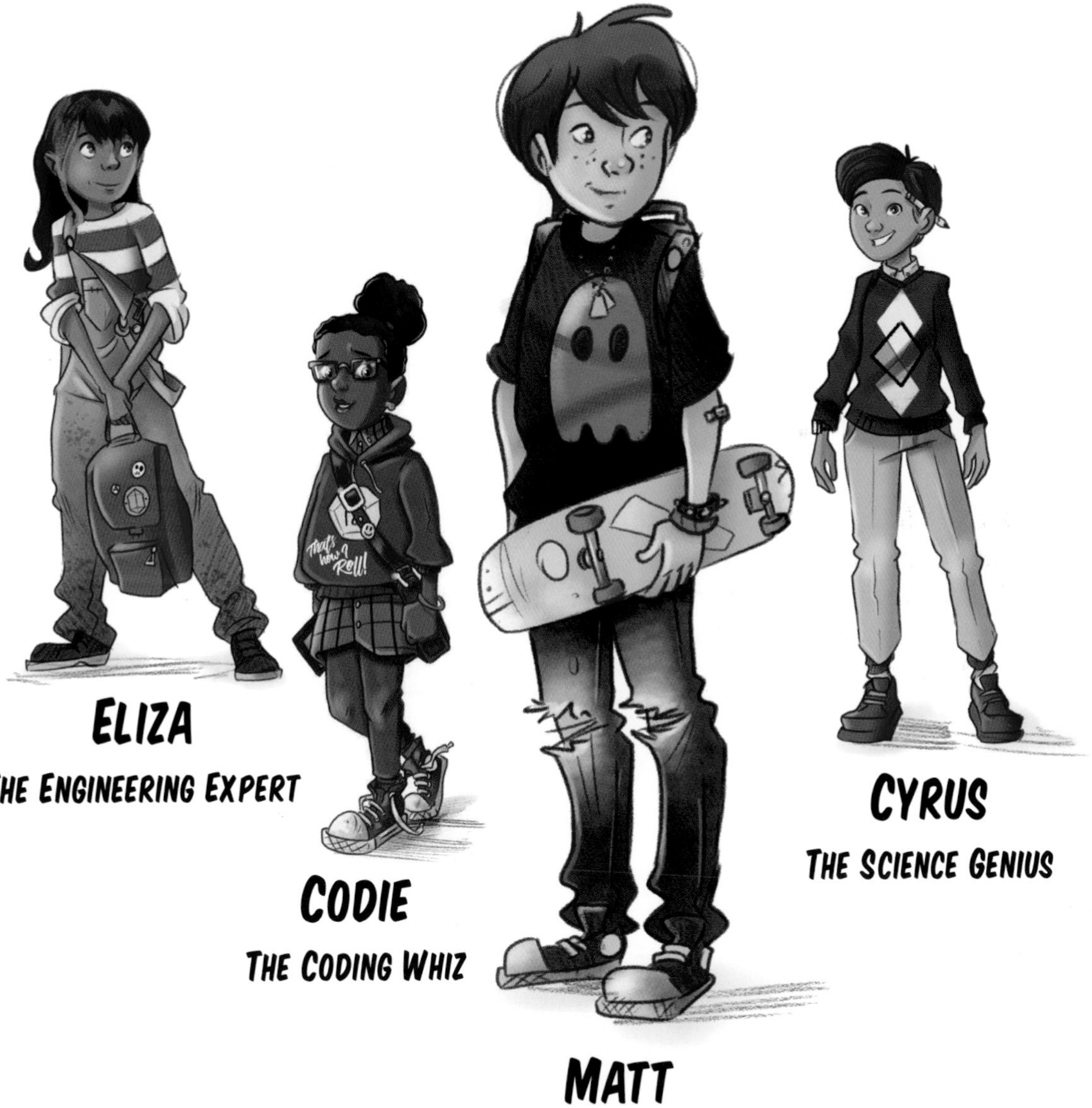
That's how I Roll!

ELIZA
THE ENGINEERING EXPERT

CODIE
THE CODING WHIZ

MATT
THE MATH MASTER

CYRUS
THE SCIENCE GENIUS

A COOL SURPRISE

TODAY, MATT AND HIS FRIENDS ARE IN THEIR FAVORITE PLACE IN ALL OF EMERSON ELEMENTARY. AT THE BACK OF THE SCHOOL'S LIBRARY IS AN AREA THAT MS. GILLIAN CALLS THE MAKERSPACE.

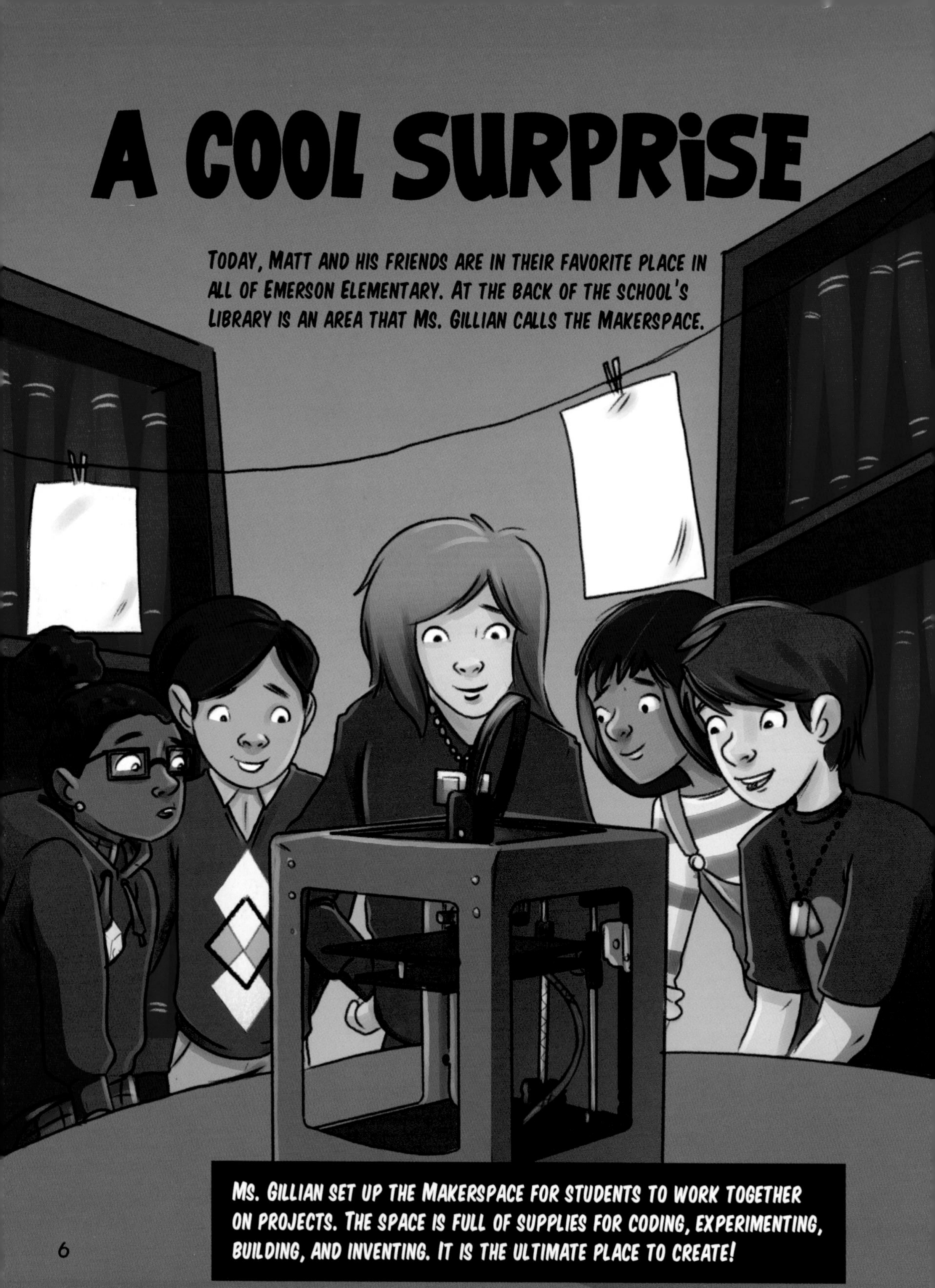

MS. GILLIAN SET UP THE MAKERSPACE FOR STUDENTS TO WORK TOGETHER ON PROJECTS. THE SPACE IS FULL OF SUPPLIES FOR CODING, EXPERIMENTING, BUILDING, AND INVENTING. IT IS THE ULTIMATE PLACE TO CREATE!

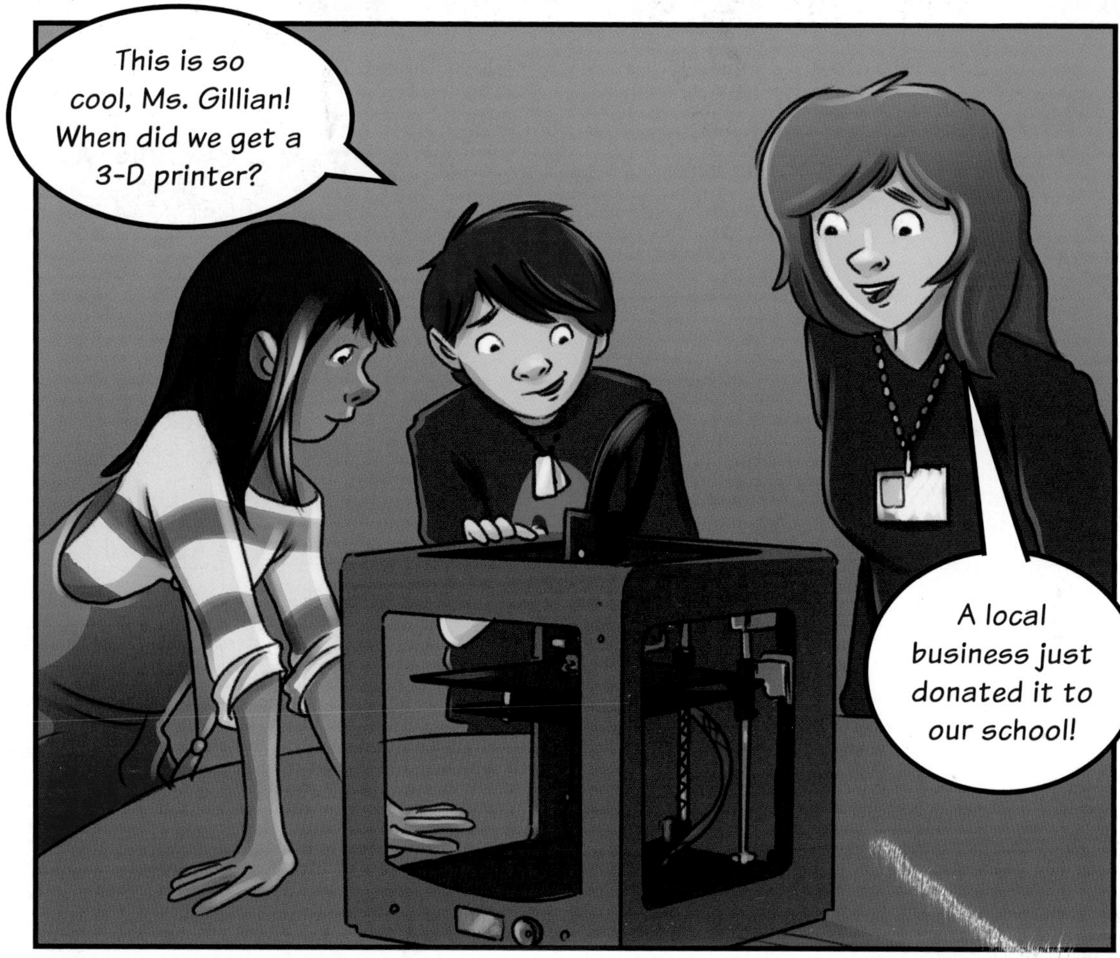
This is so cool, Ms. Gillian! When did we get a 3-D printer?
A local business just donated it to our school!

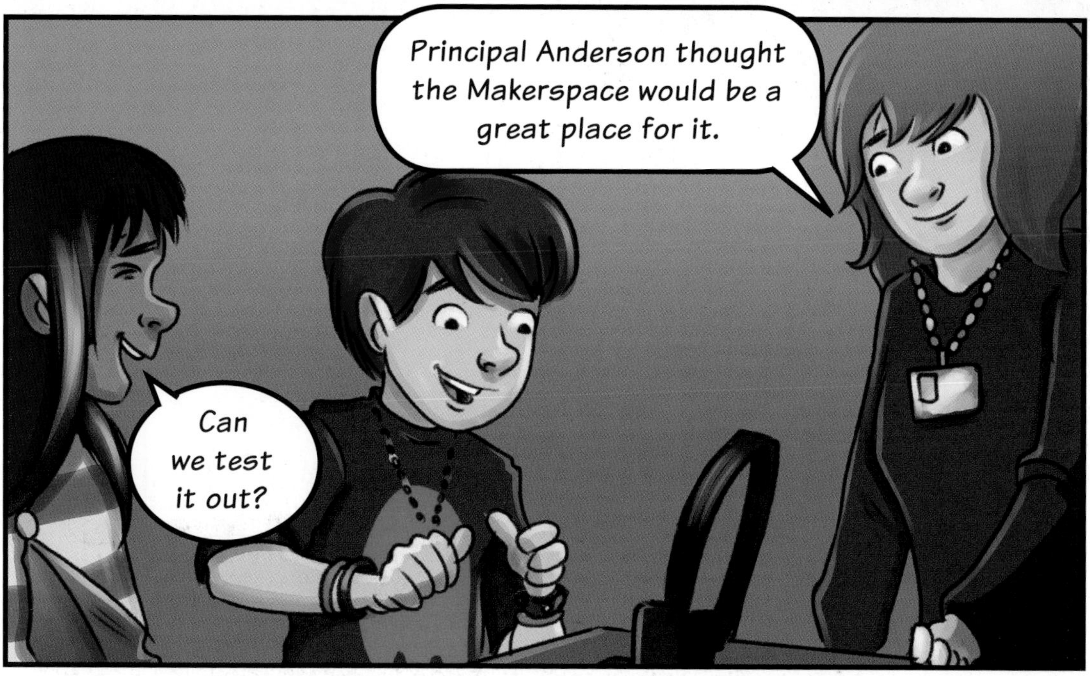
Principal Anderson thought the Makerspace would be a great place for it.
Can we test it out?

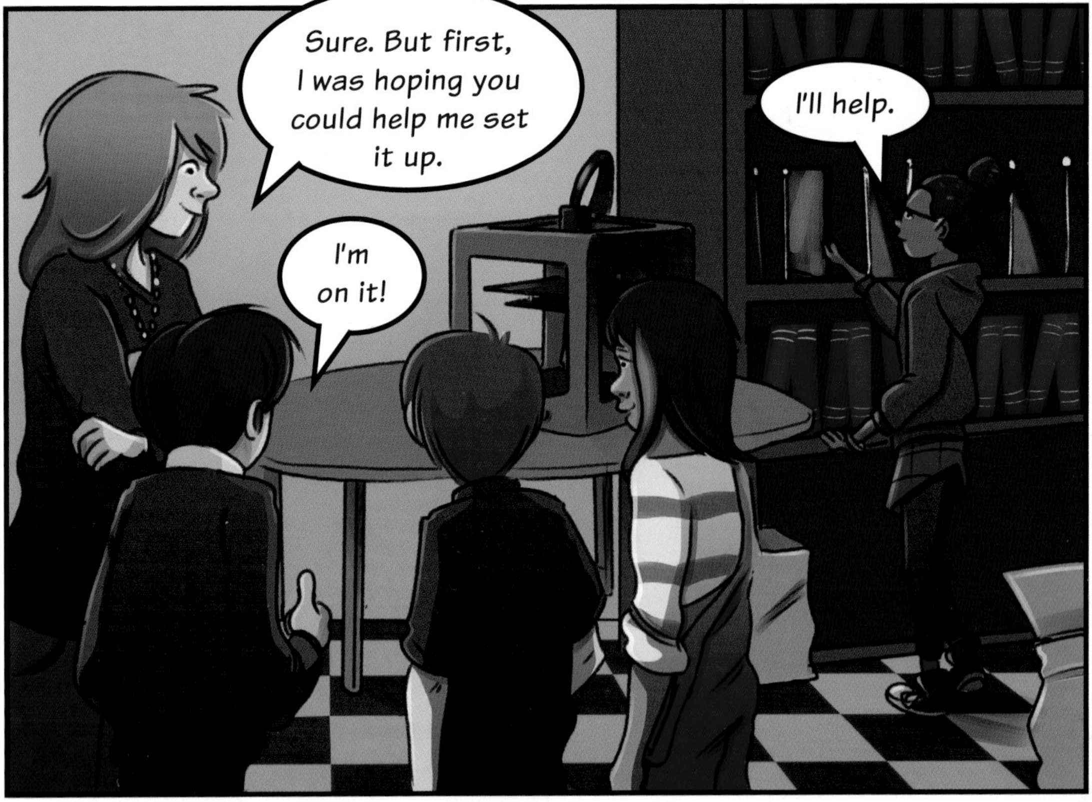
Sure. But first, I was hoping you could help me set it up.
I'm on it!
I'll help.

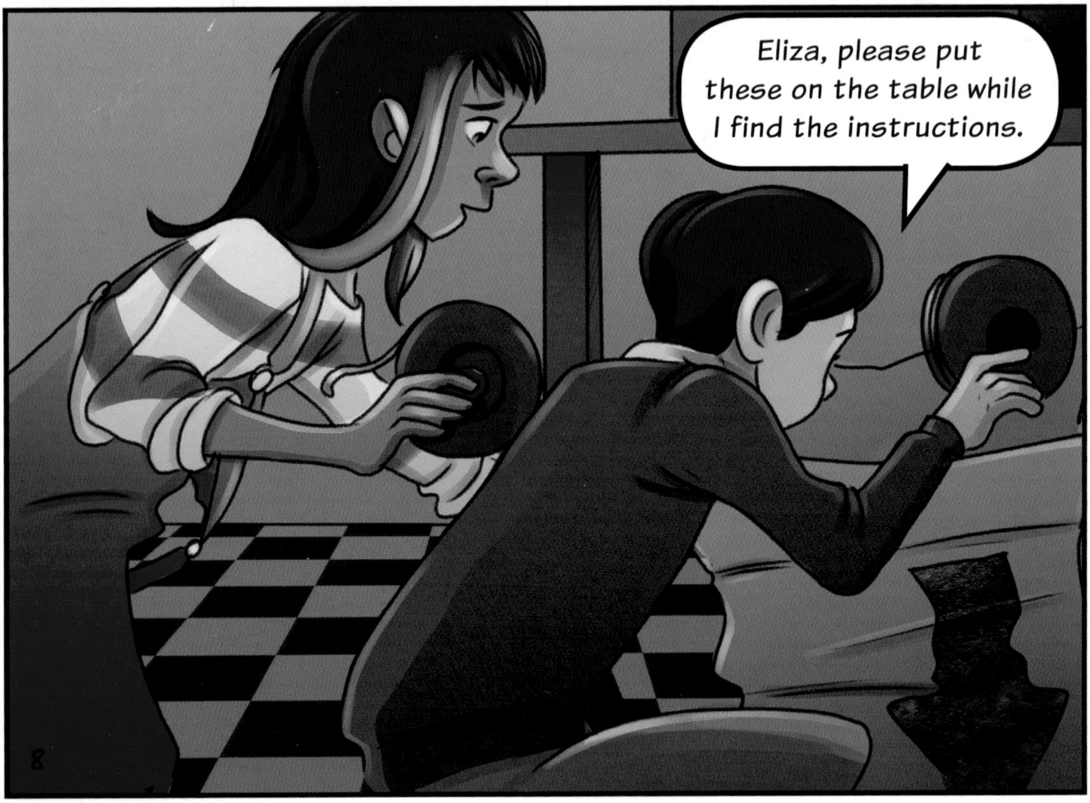
Eliza, please put these on the table while I find the instructions.

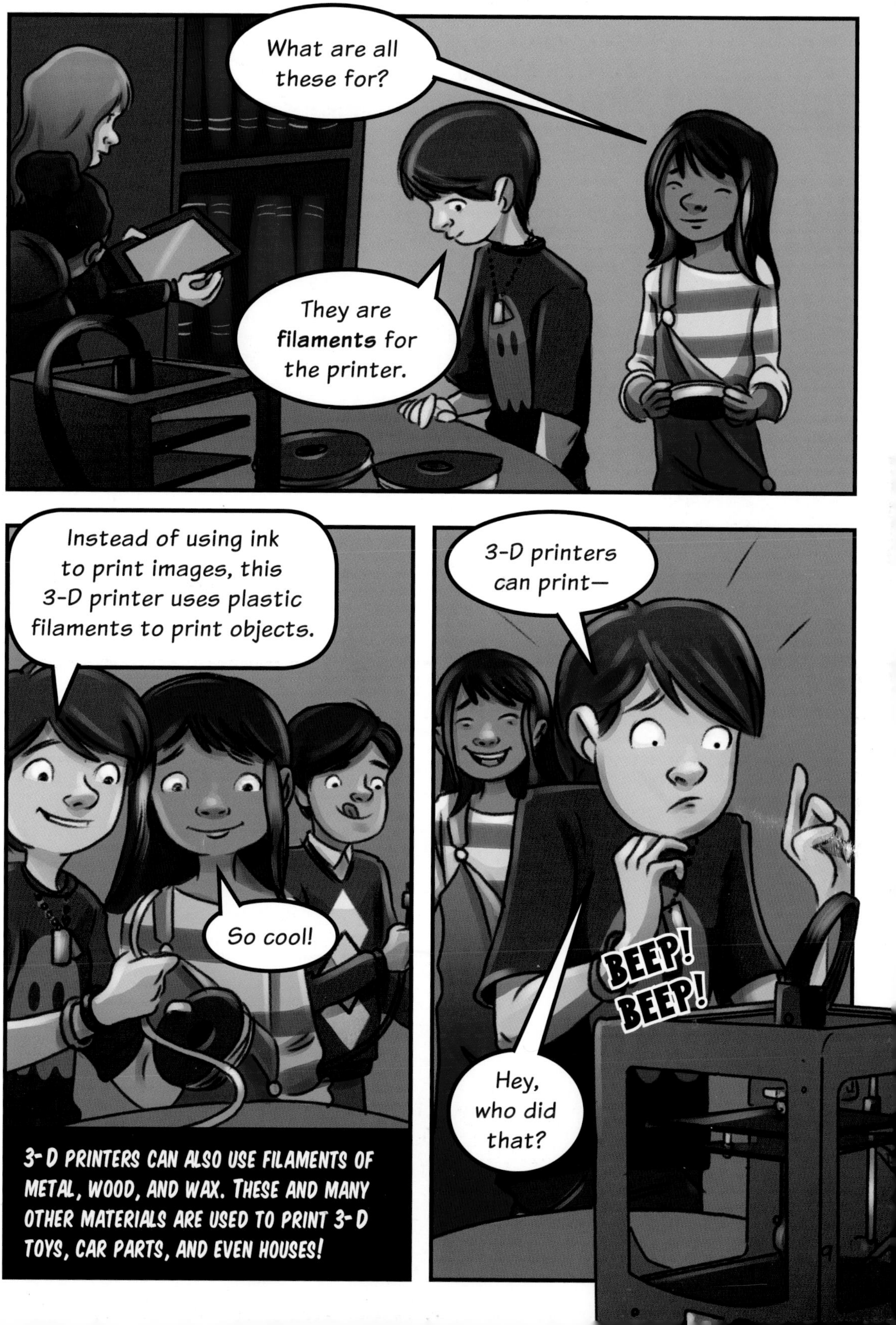
What are all these for?
They are **filaments** for the printer.
Instead of using ink to print images, this 3-D printer uses plastic filaments to print objects.
So cool!
3-D PRINTERS CAN ALSO USE FILAMENTS OF METAL, WOOD, AND WAX. THESE AND MANY OTHER MATERIALS ARE USED TO PRINT 3-D TOYS, CAR PARTS, AND EVEN HOUSES!
3-D printers can print—
BEEP! BEEP!
Hey, who did that?

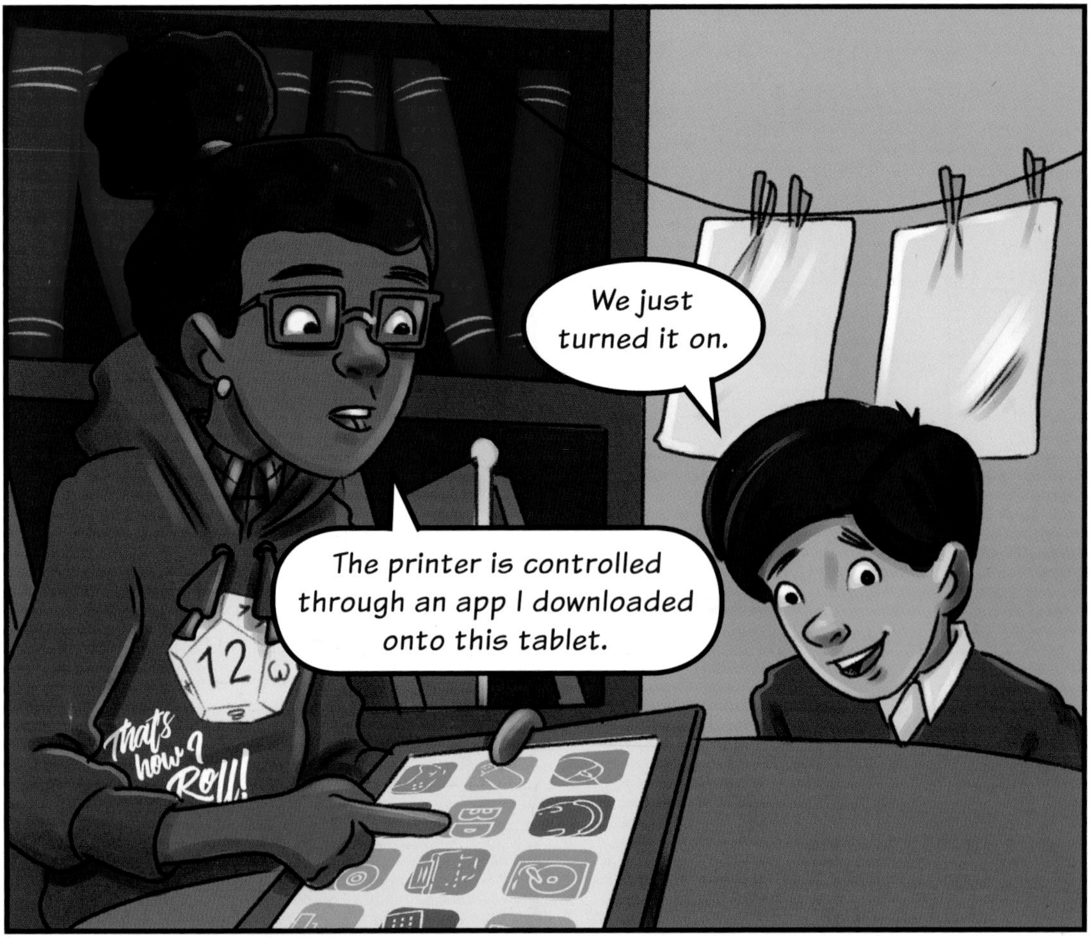
We just turned it on.
The printer is controlled through an app I downloaded onto this tablet.
12
That's how I Roll!

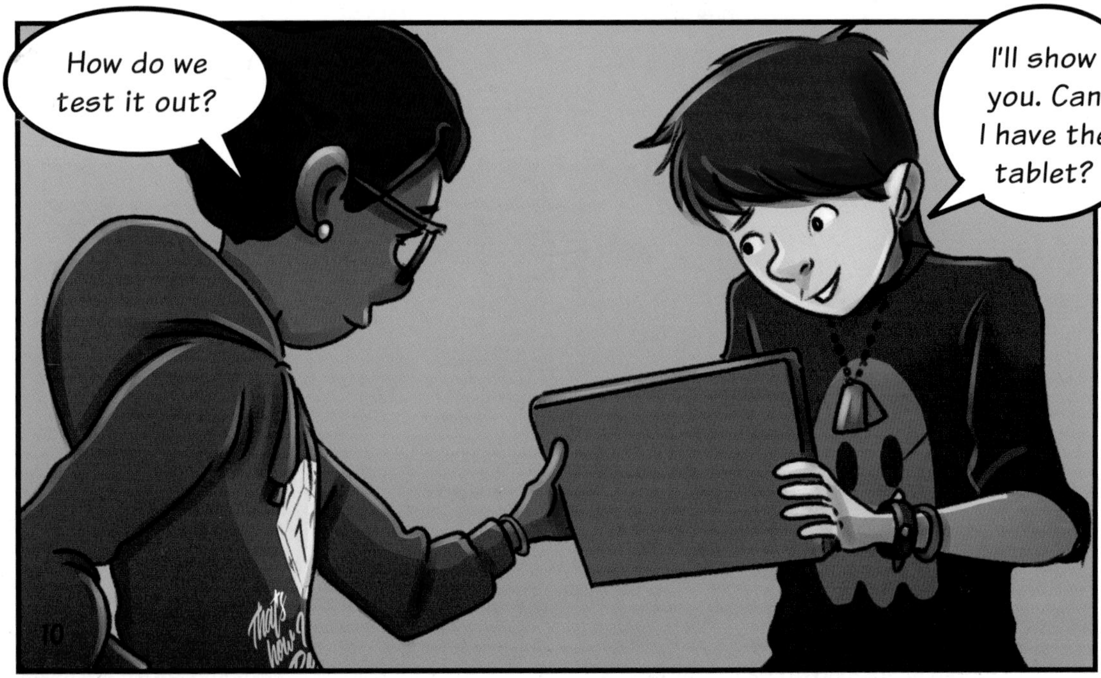
How do we test it out?
I'll show you. Can I have the tablet?

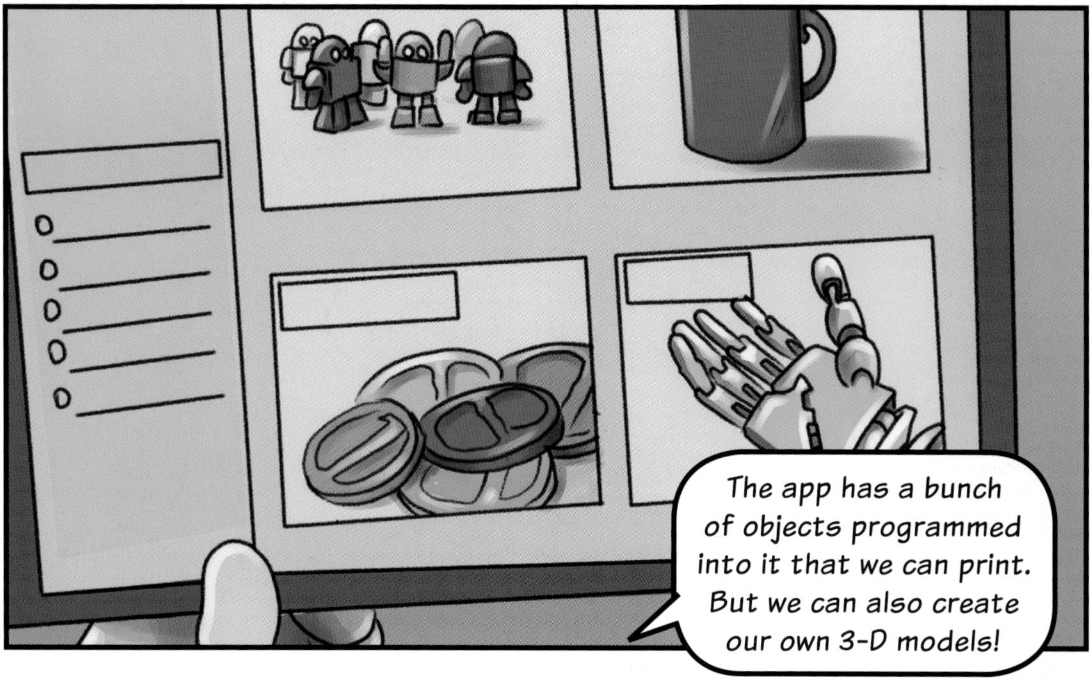
The app has a bunch of objects programmed into it that we can print. But we can also create our own 3-D models!

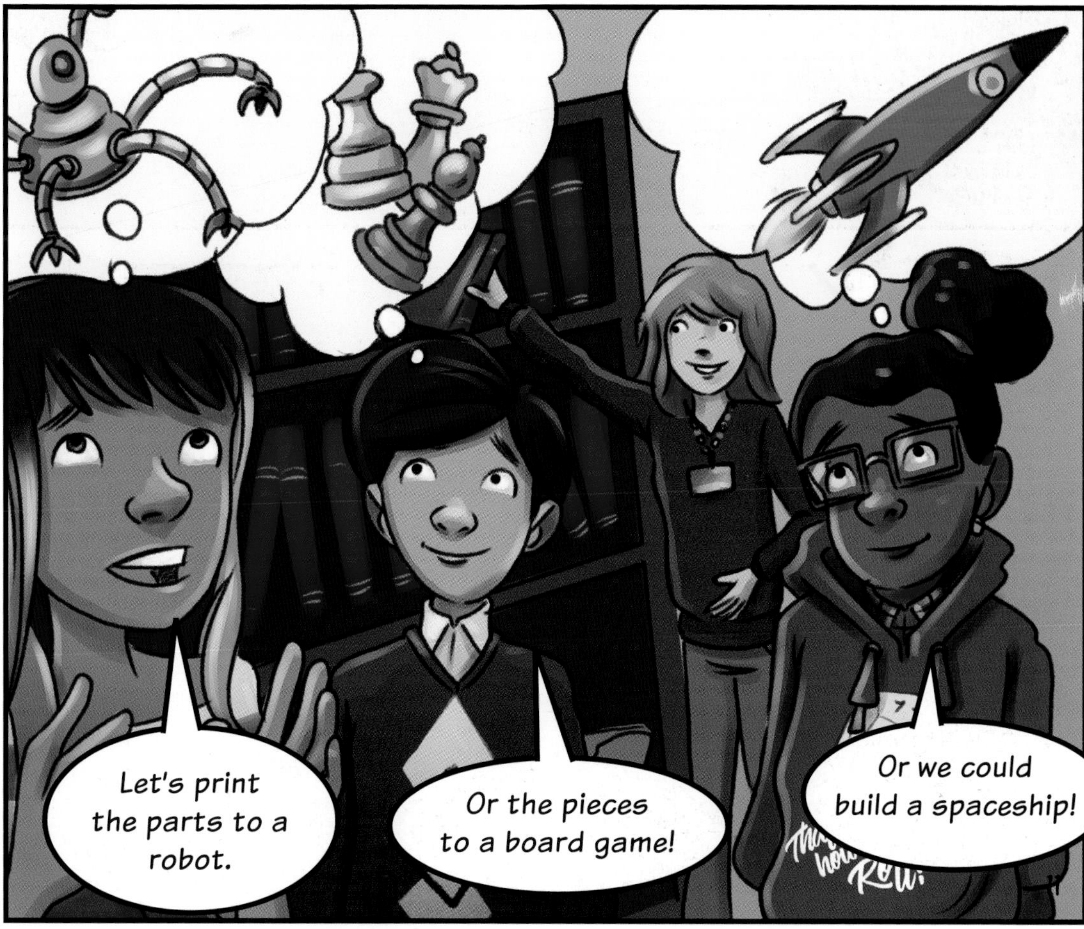
Let's print the parts to a robot.
Or the pieces to a board game!
Or we could build a spaceship!

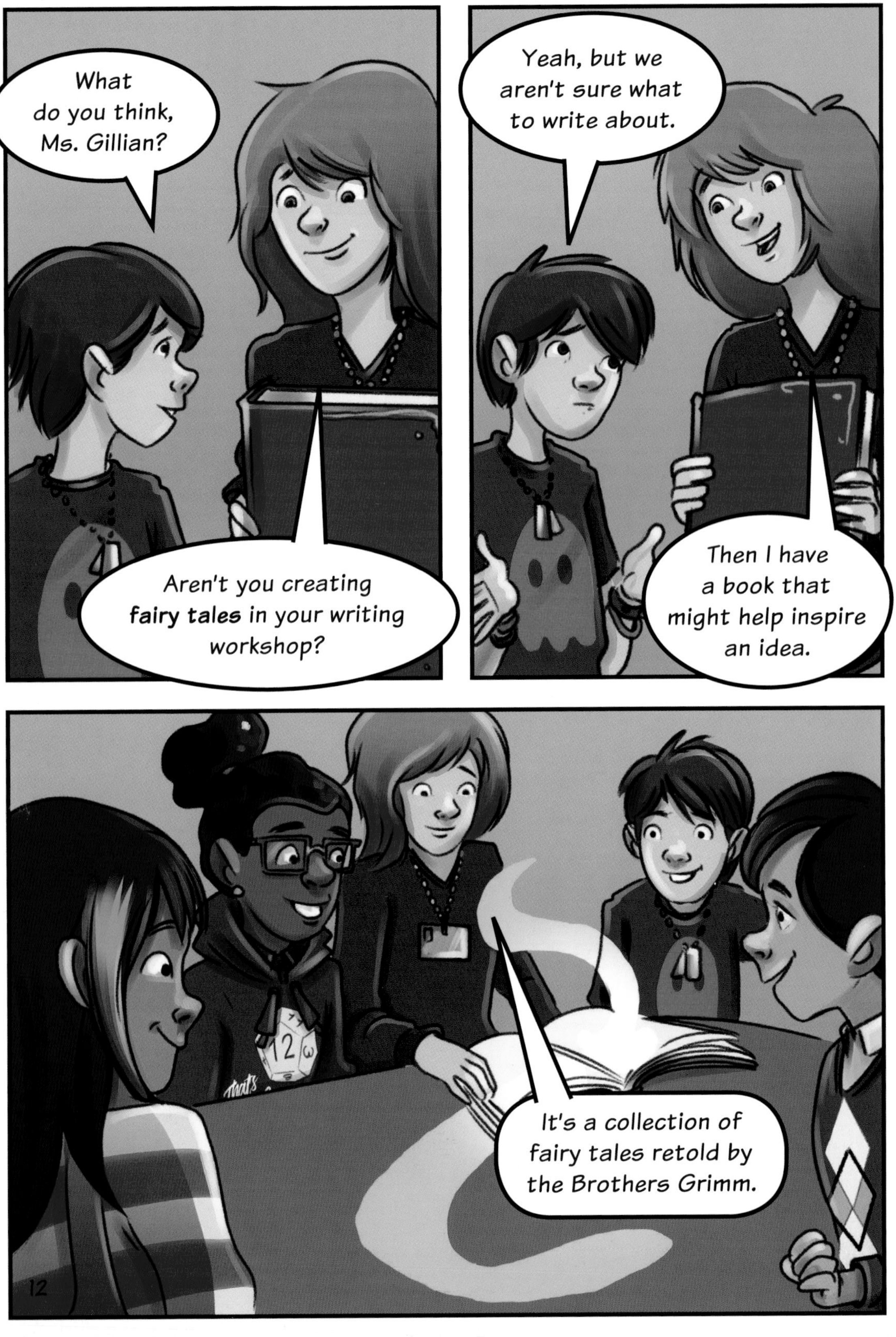
What do you think, Ms. Gillian?
Aren't you creating **fairy tales** in your writing workshop?
Yeah, but we aren't sure what to write about.
Then I have a book that might help inspire an idea.
It's a collection of fairy tales retold by the Brothers Grimm.

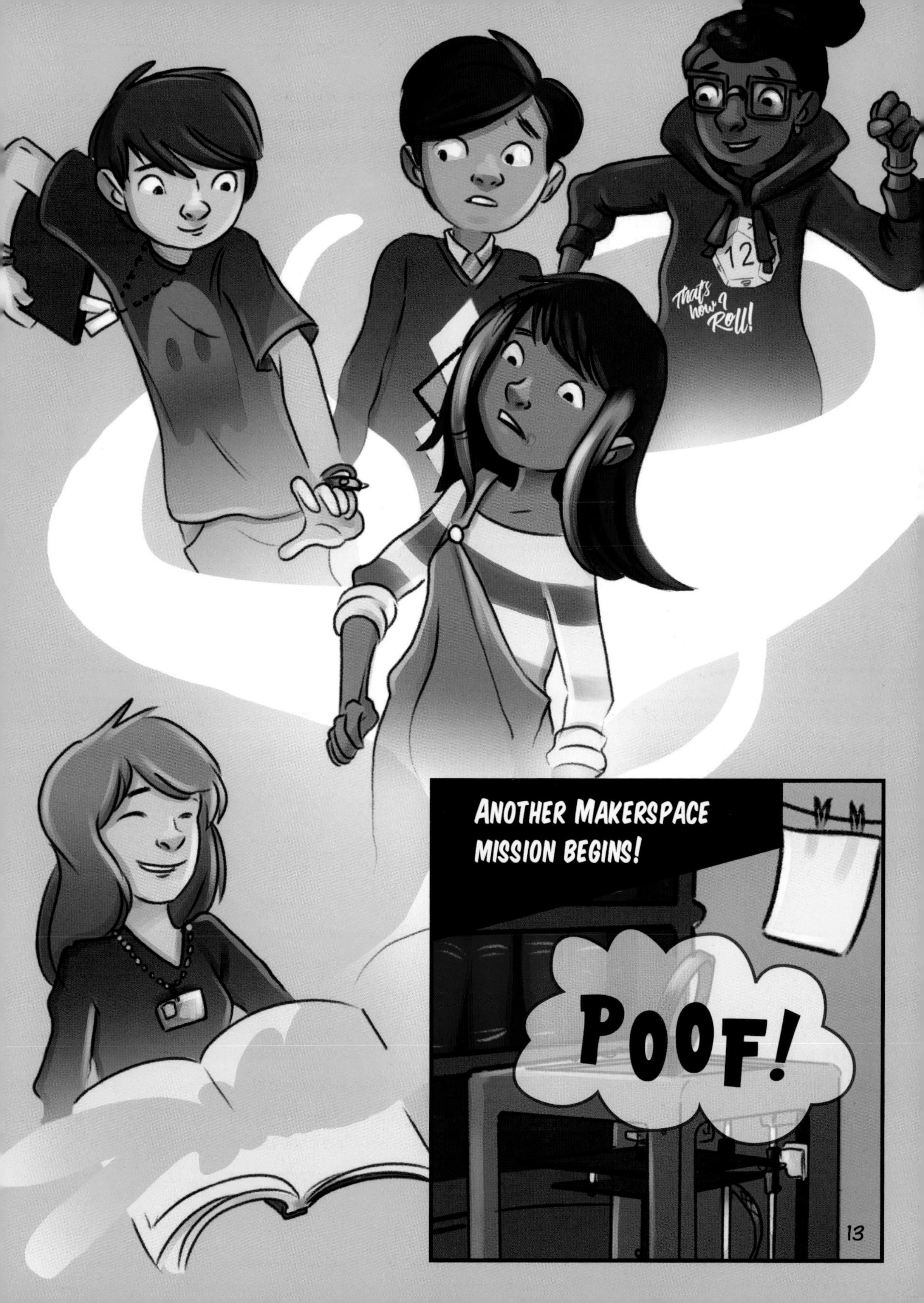

That's how I Roll!
12
ANOTHER MAKERSPACE MISSION BEGINS!
POOF!

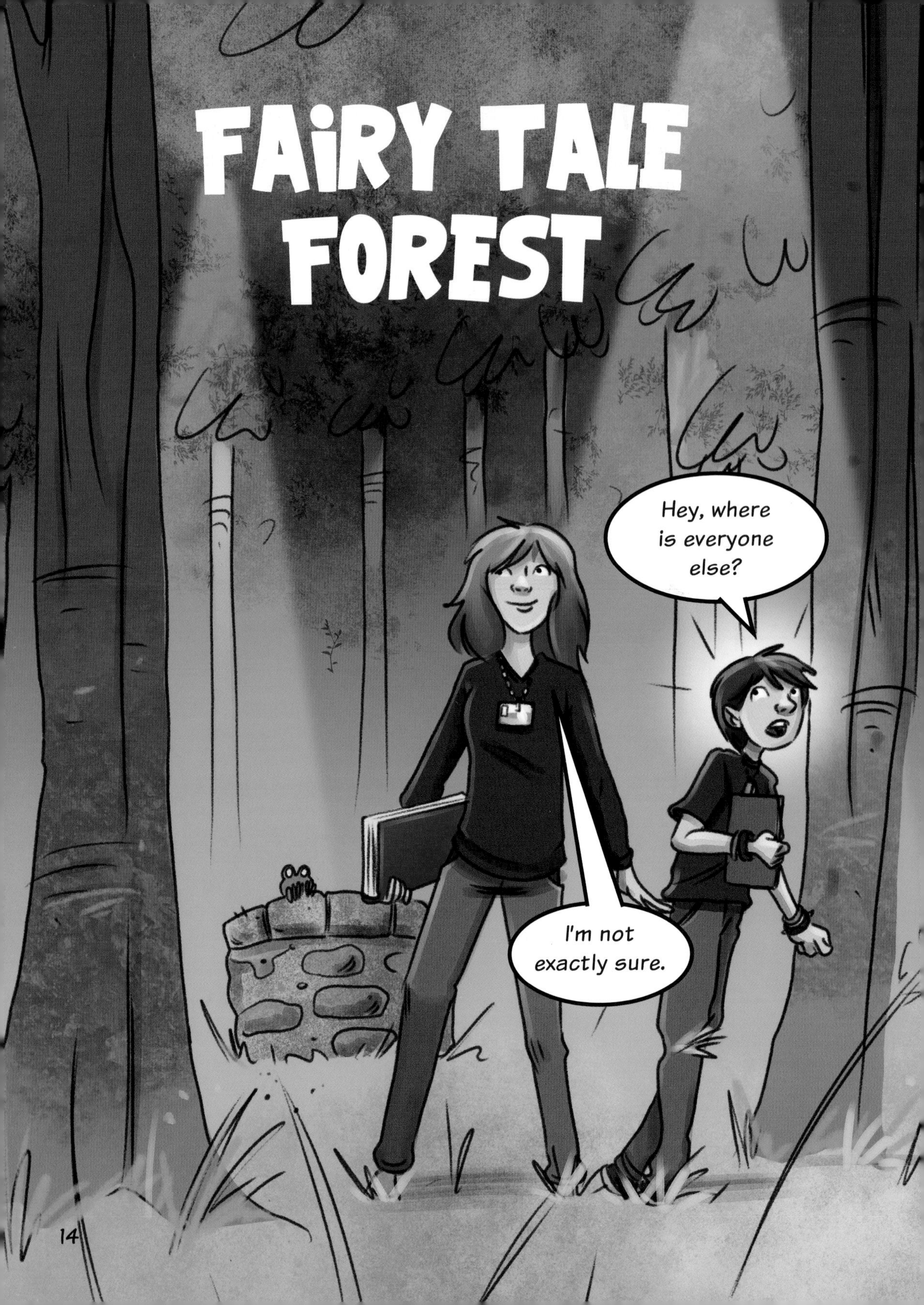
FAIRY TALE FOREST
Hey, where is everyone else?
I'm not exactly sure.

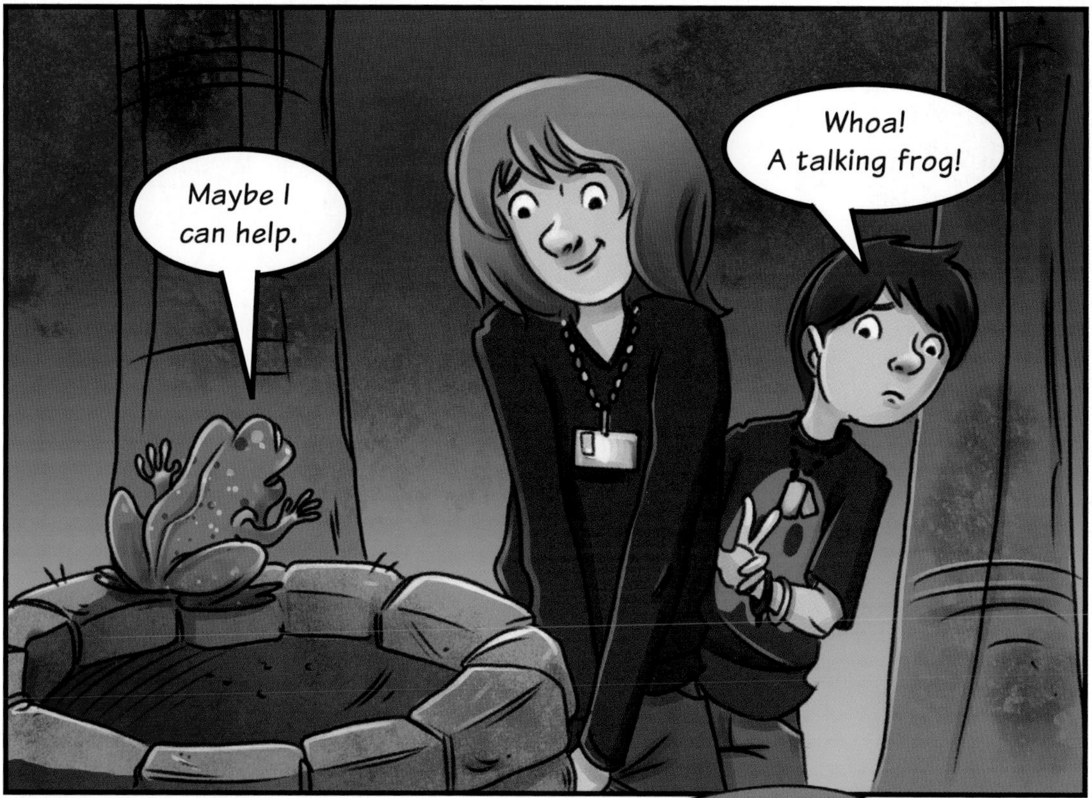
Maybe I can help.
Whoa! A talking frog!

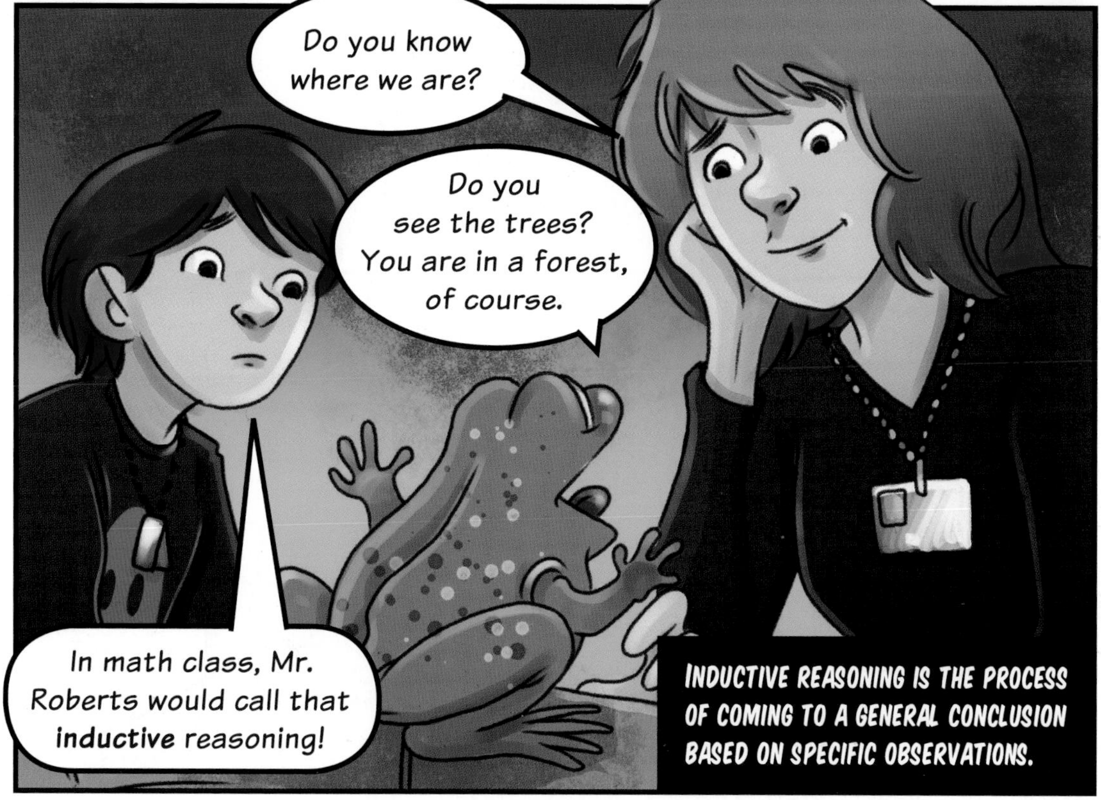
Do you know where we are?
Do you see the trees? You are in a forest, of course.
In math class, Mr. Roberts would call that **inductive** reasoning!
INDUCTIVE REASONING IS THE PROCESS OF COMING TO A GENERAL CONCLUSION BASED ON SPECIFIC OBSERVATIONS.

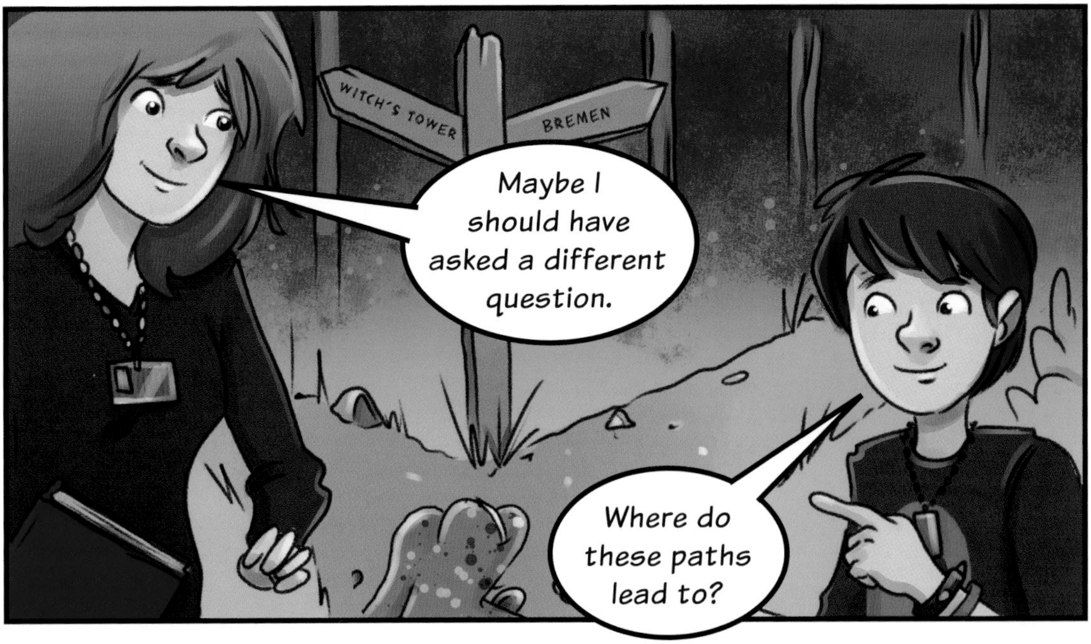
WITCH'S TOWER
BREMEN
Where do these paths lead to?
Maybe I should have asked a different question.

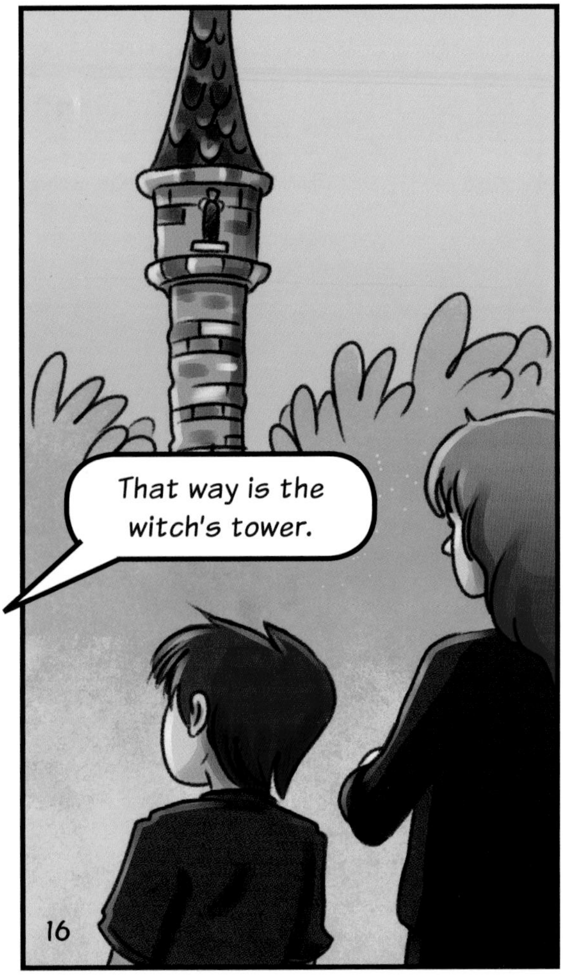
That way is the witch's tower.

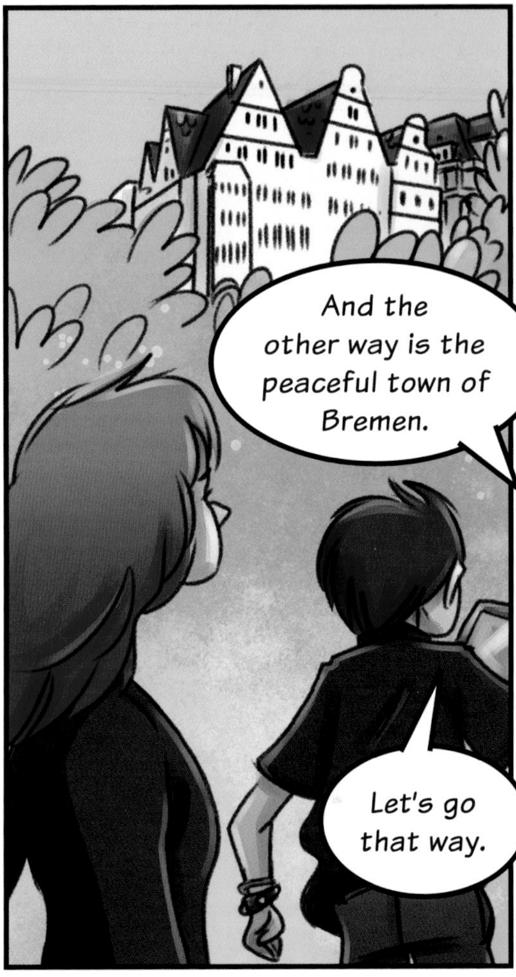
And the other way is the peaceful town of Bremen.
Let's go that way.

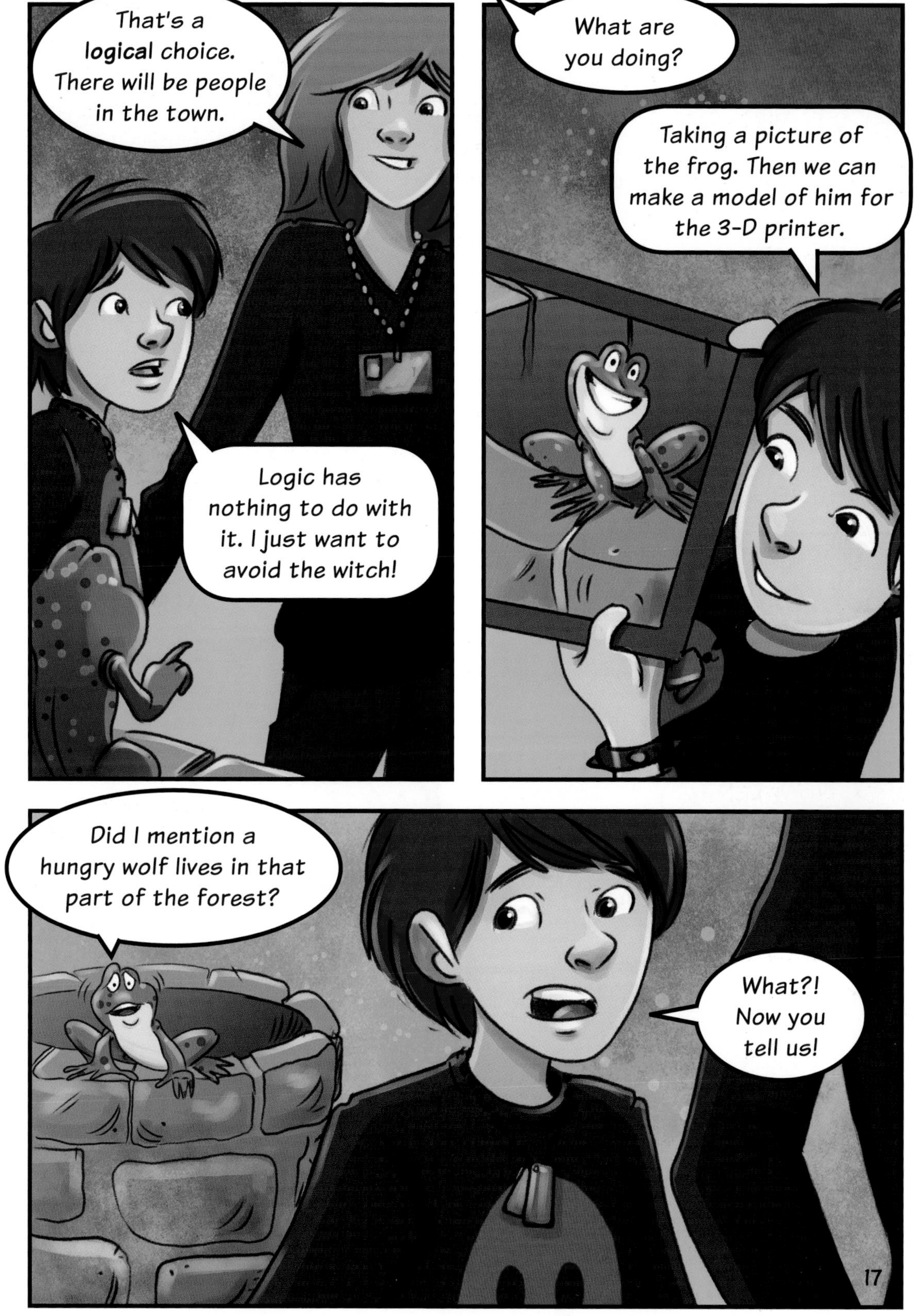
That's a **logical** choice. There will be people in the town.
Logic has nothing to do with it. I just want to avoid the witch!
What are you doing?
Taking a picture of the frog. Then we can make a model of him for the 3-D printer.
Did I mention a hungry wolf lives in that part of the forest?
What?! Now you tell us!

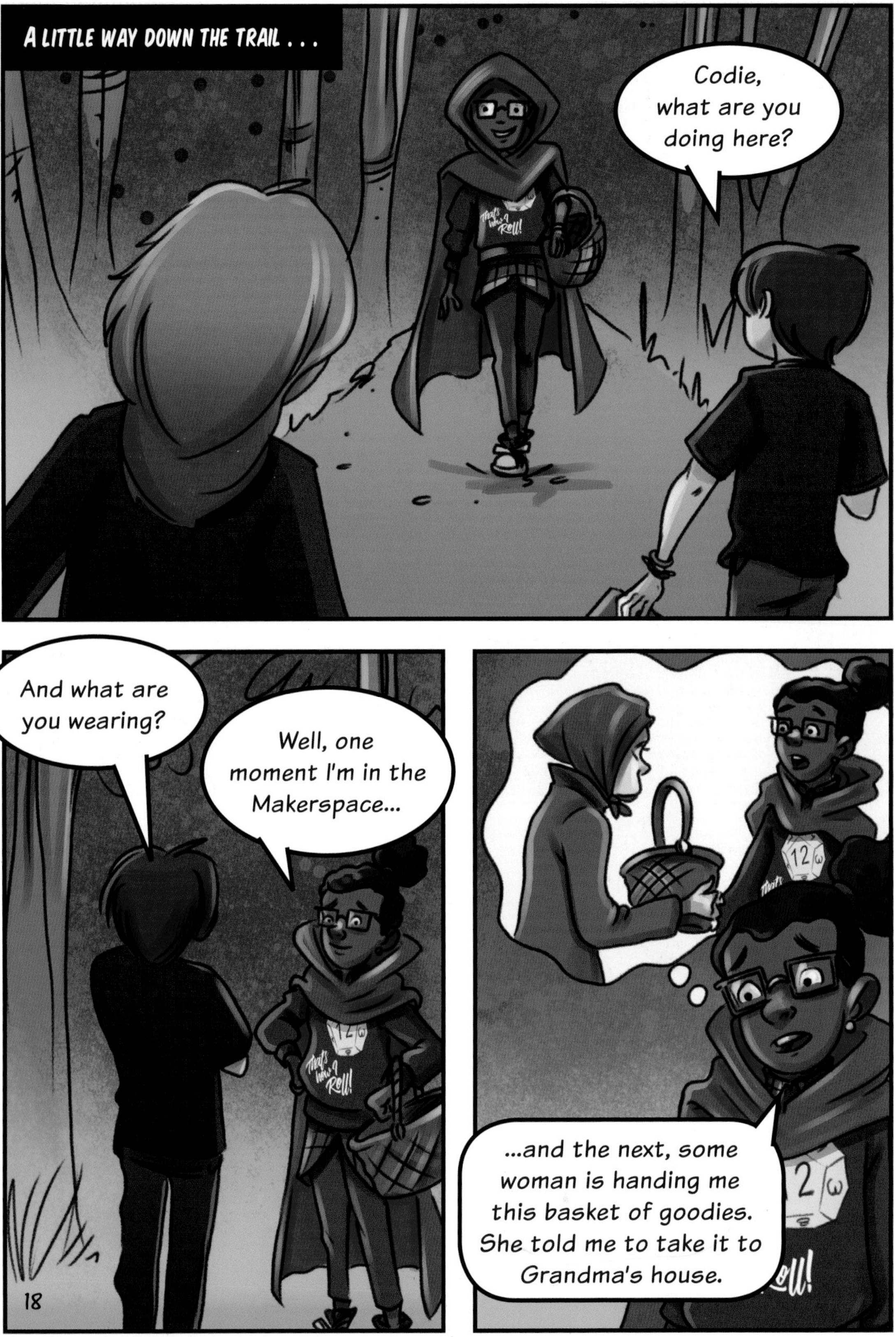
A LITTLE WAY DOWN THE TRAIL . . .
Codie, what are you doing here?
And what are you wearing?
Well, one moment I'm in the Makerspace...
...and the next, some woman is handing me this basket of goodies. She told me to take it to Grandma's house.

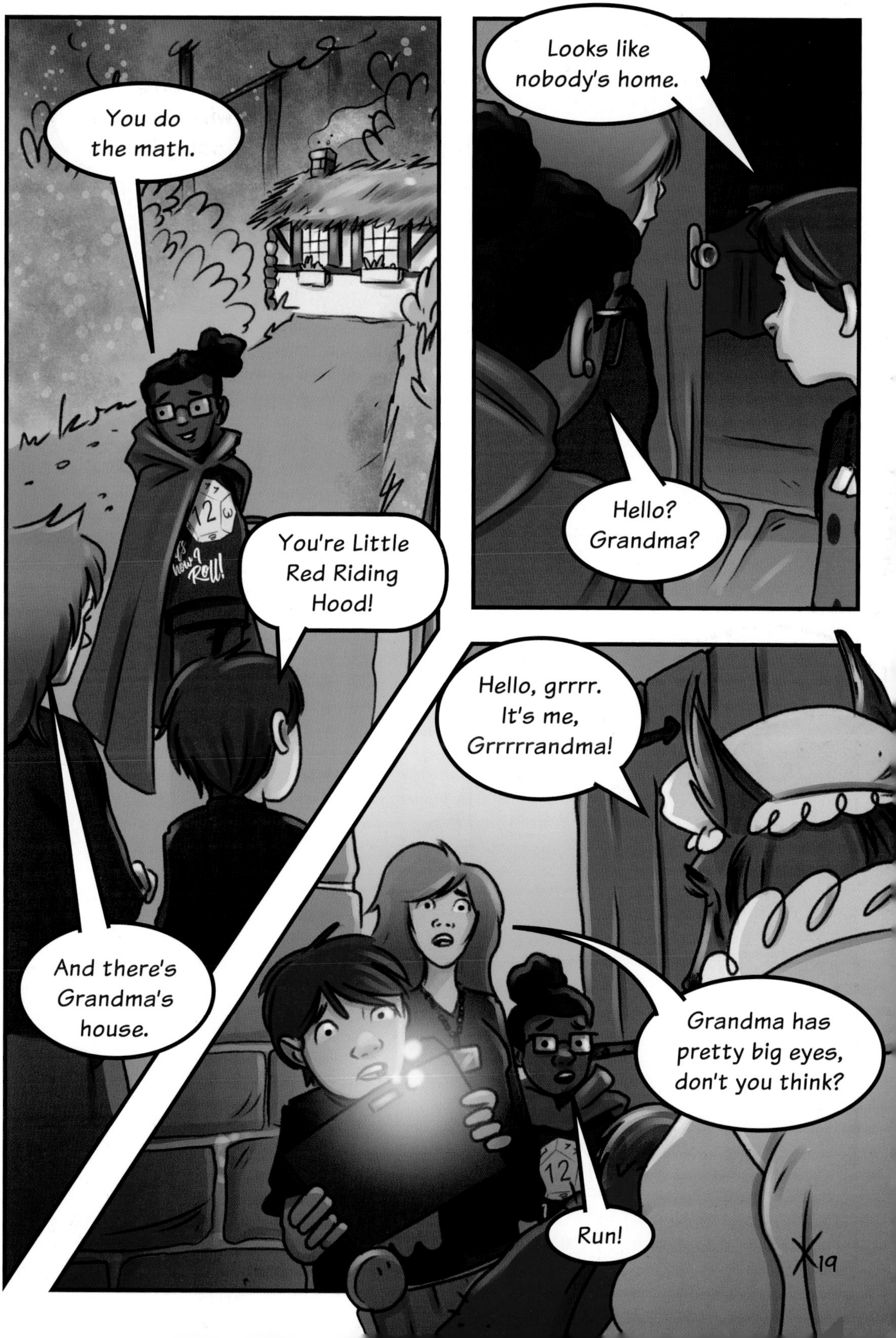
You do the math.
You're Little Red Riding Hood!
And there's Grandma's house.
Looks like nobody's home.
Hello? Grandma?
Hello, grrrr. It's me, Grrrrrandma!
Grandma has pretty big eyes, don't you think?
Run!
19

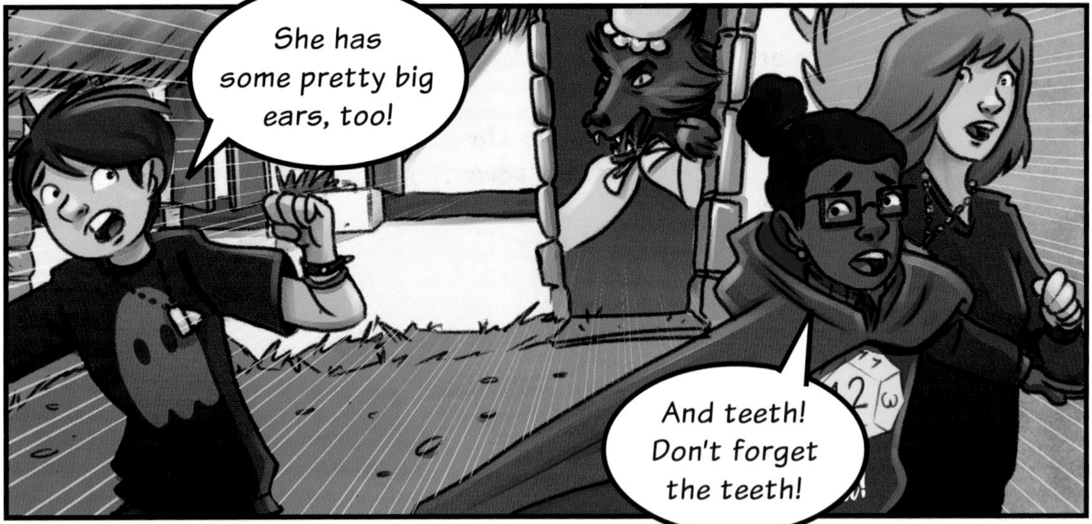
She has some pretty big ears, too!
And teeth! Don't forget the teeth!

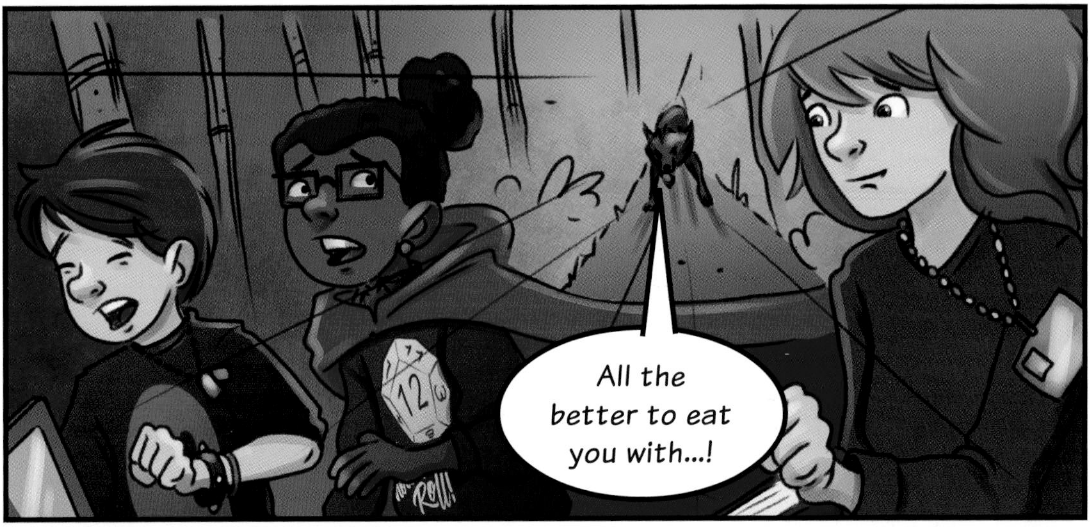
All the better to eat you with...!

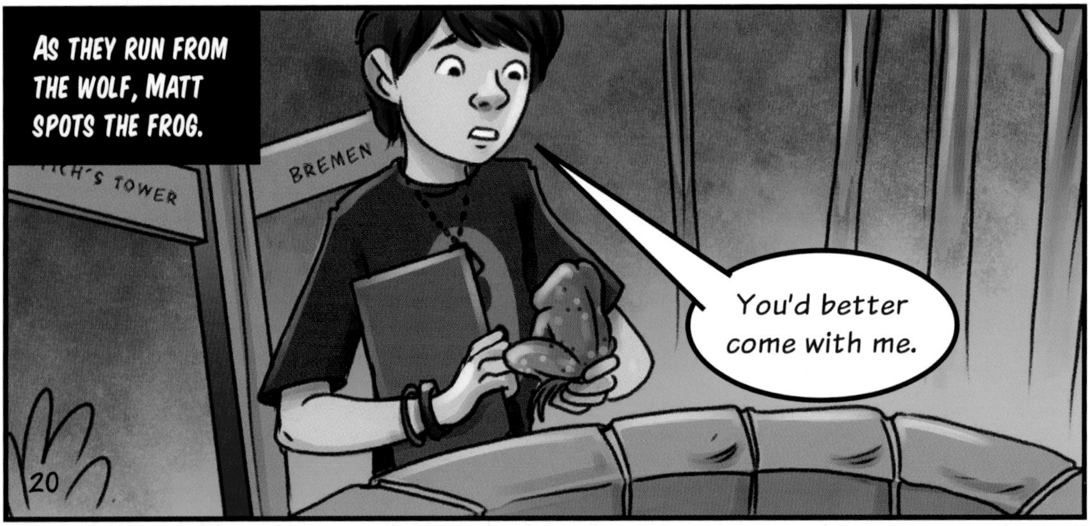
AS THEY RUN FROM THE WOLF, MATT SPOTS THE FROG.
BREMEN
You'd better come with me.

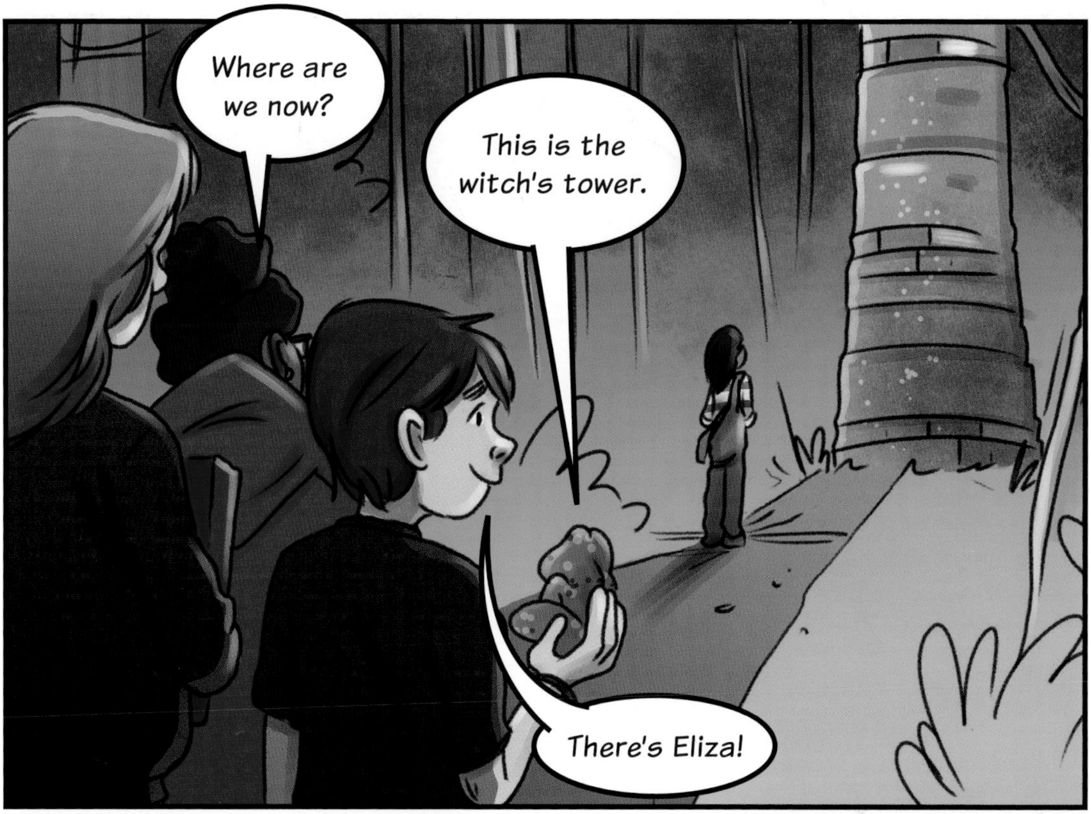
Where are we now?
This is the witch's tower.
There's Eliza!

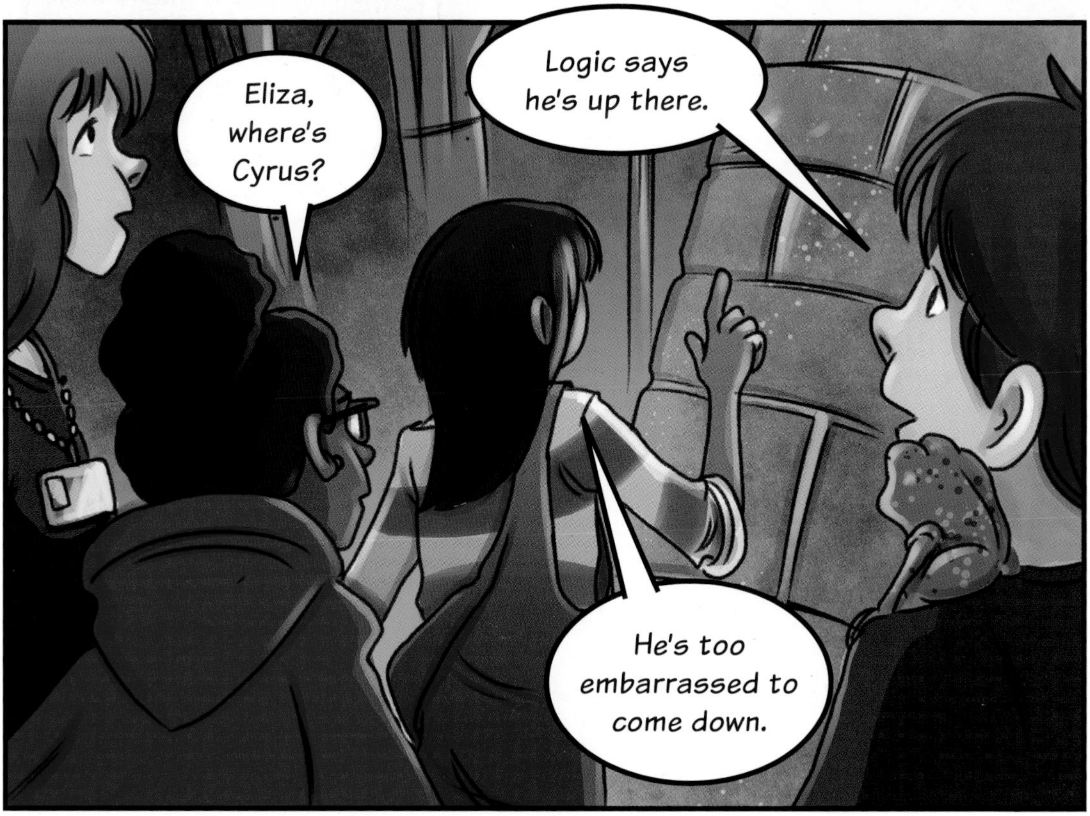
Eliza, where's Cyrus?
Logic says he's up there.
He's too embarrassed to come down.

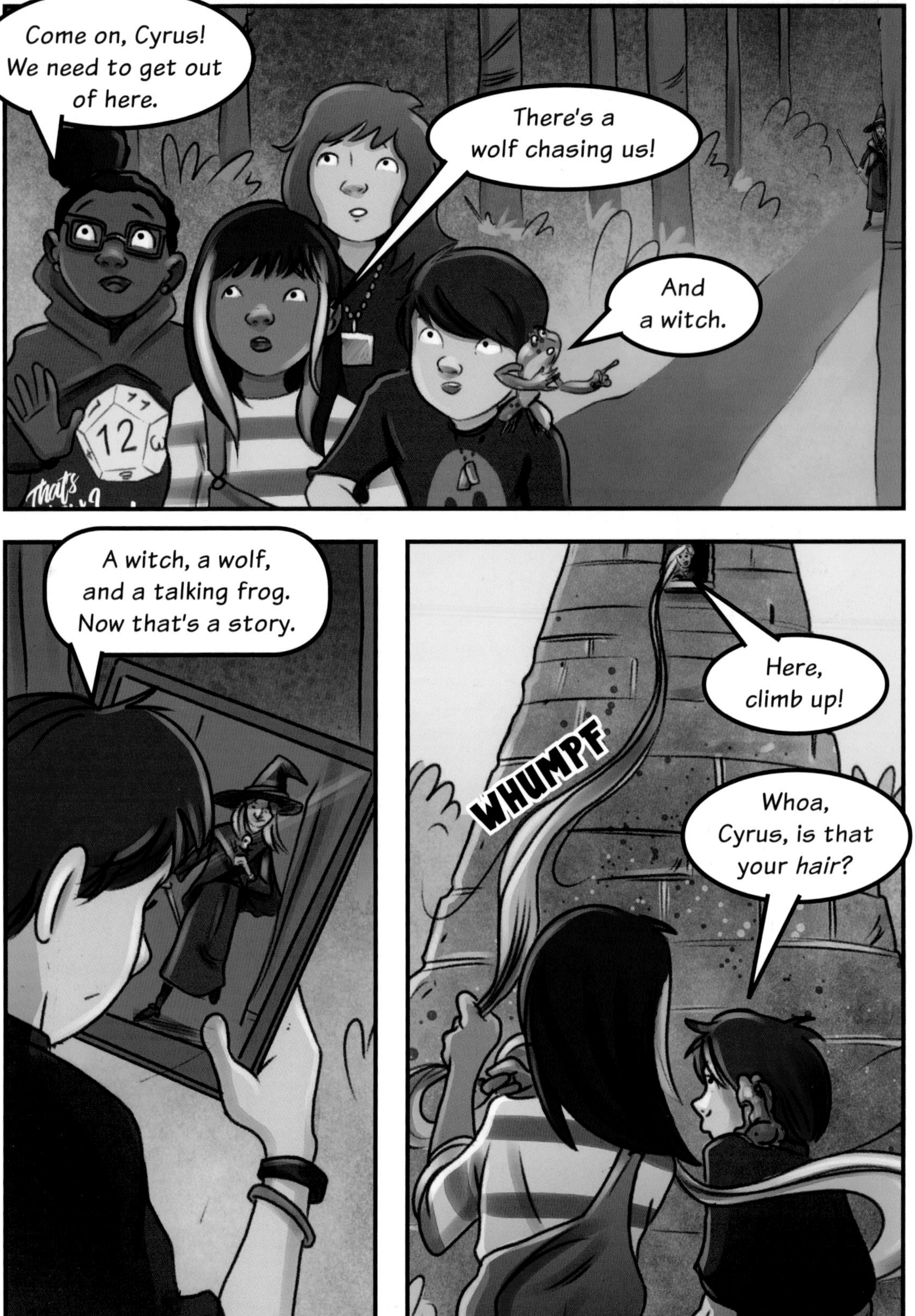
Come on, Cyrus! We need to get out of here.
There's a wolf chasing us!
And a witch.
A witch, a wolf, and a talking frog. Now that's a story.
Here, climb up!
WHUMPF
Whoa, Cyrus, is that your *hair*?

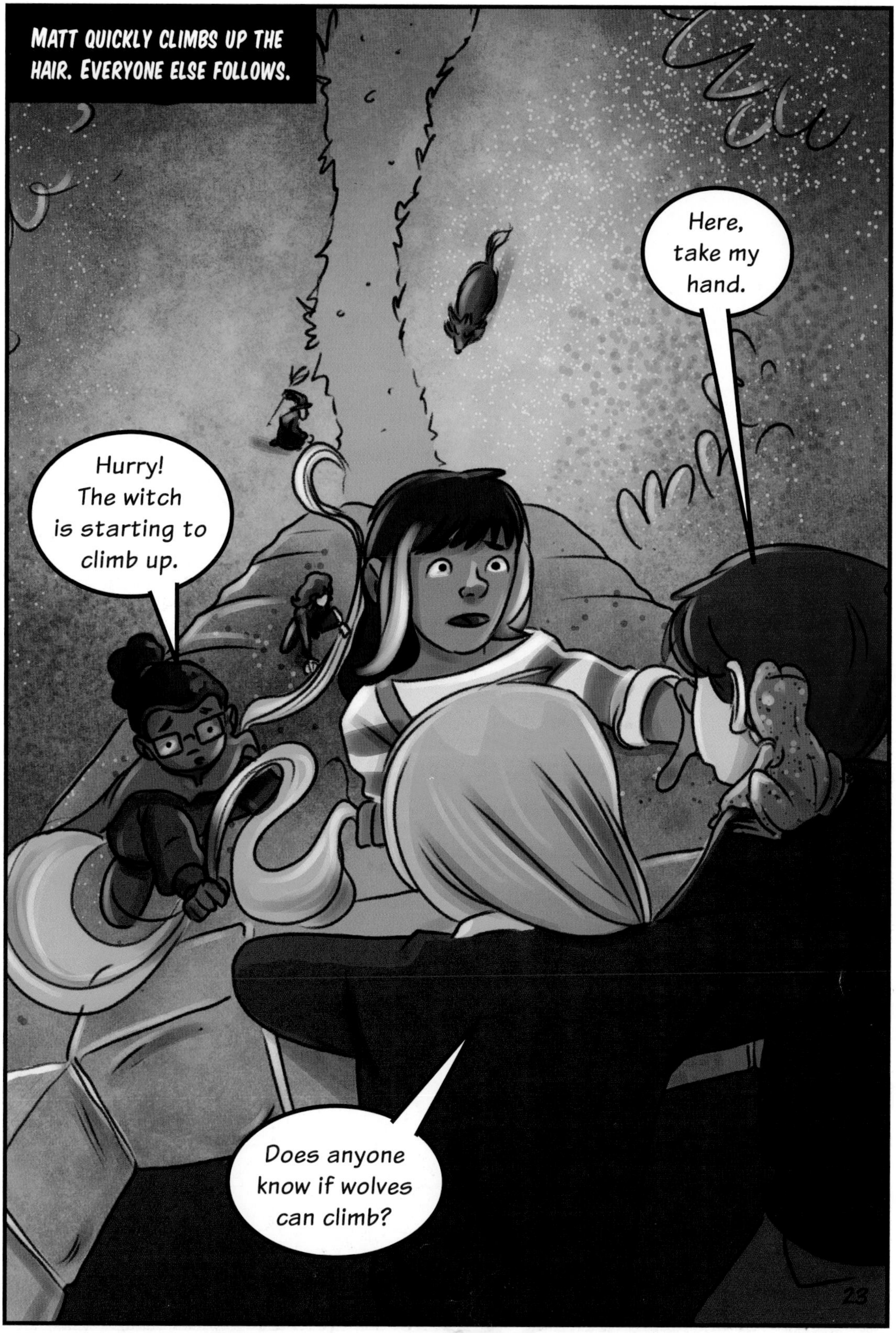
MATT QUICKLY CLIMBS UP THE HAIR. EVERYONE ELSE FOLLOWS.
Hurry! The witch is starting to climb up.
Here, take my hand.
Does anyone know if wolves can climb?

THE REAL WORLD

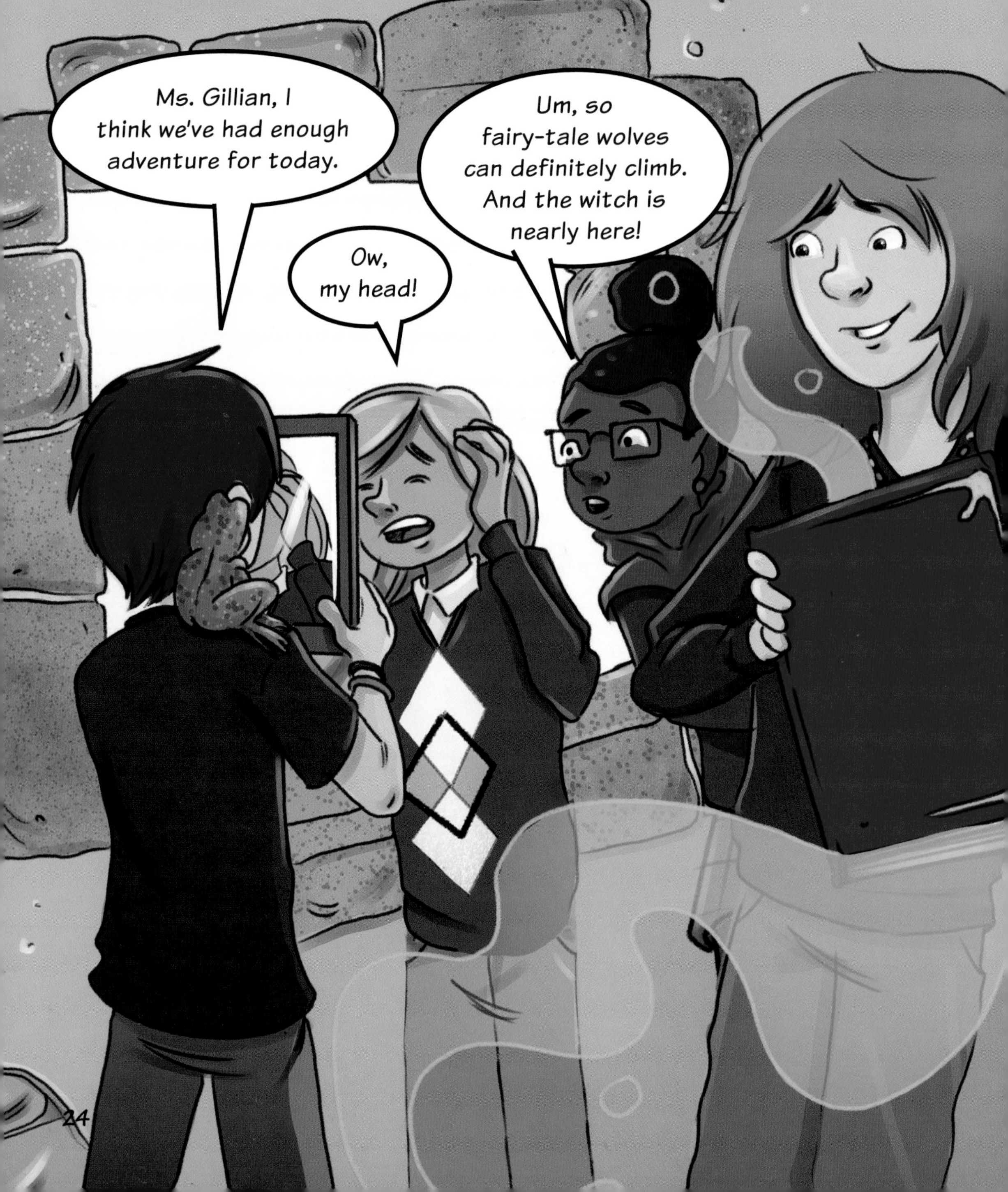
Ms. Gillian, I think we've had enough adventure for today.
Ow, my head!
Um, so fairy-tale wolves can definitely climb. And the witch is nearly here!

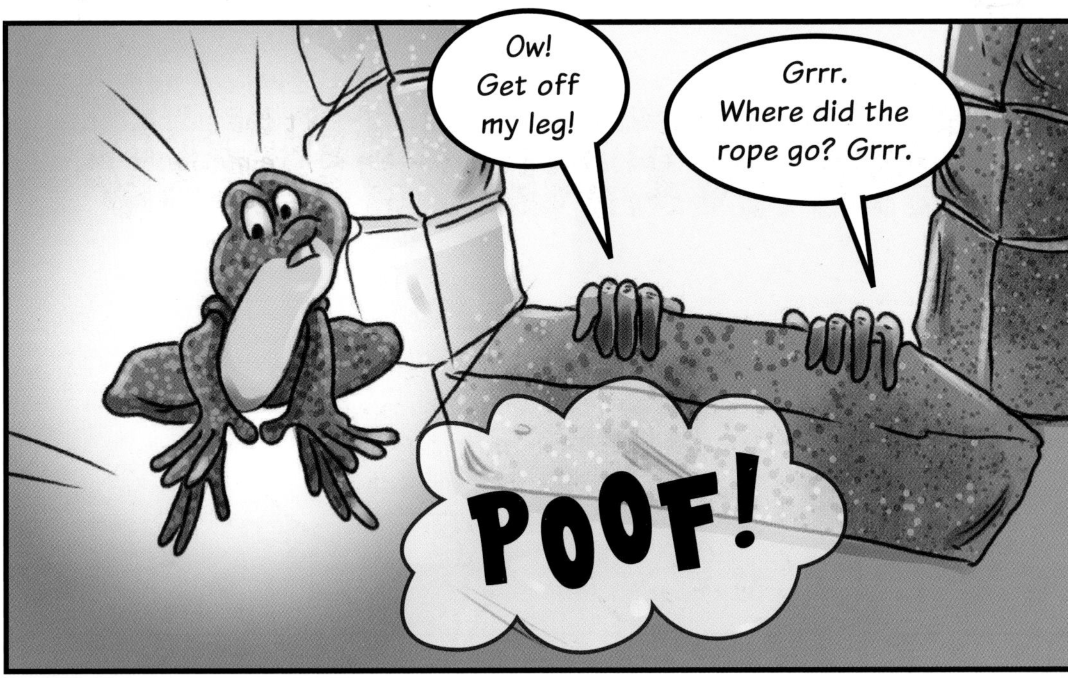
Ow! Get off my leg!
Grrr. Where did the rope go? Grrr.
POOF!

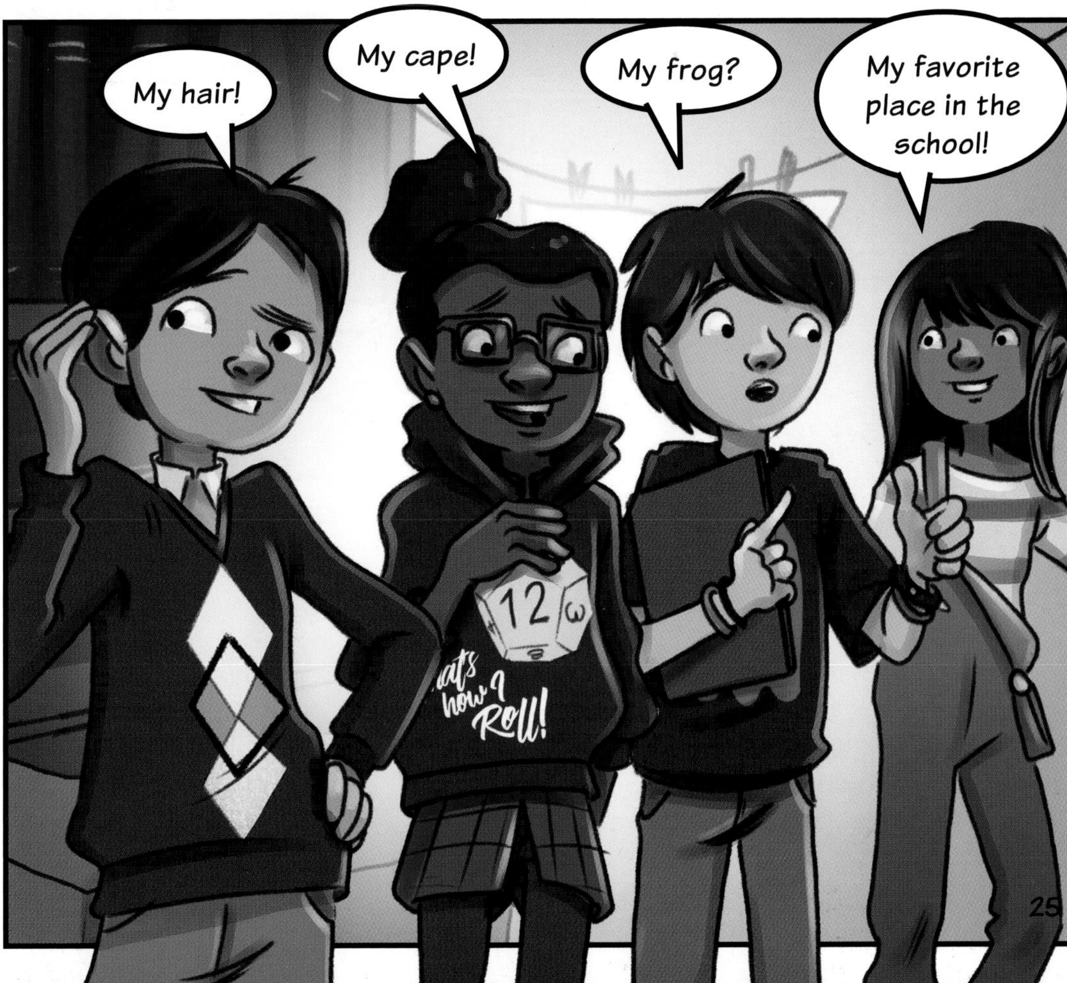
My hair!
My cape!
My frog?
My favorite place in the school!
12
hats how I Roll!

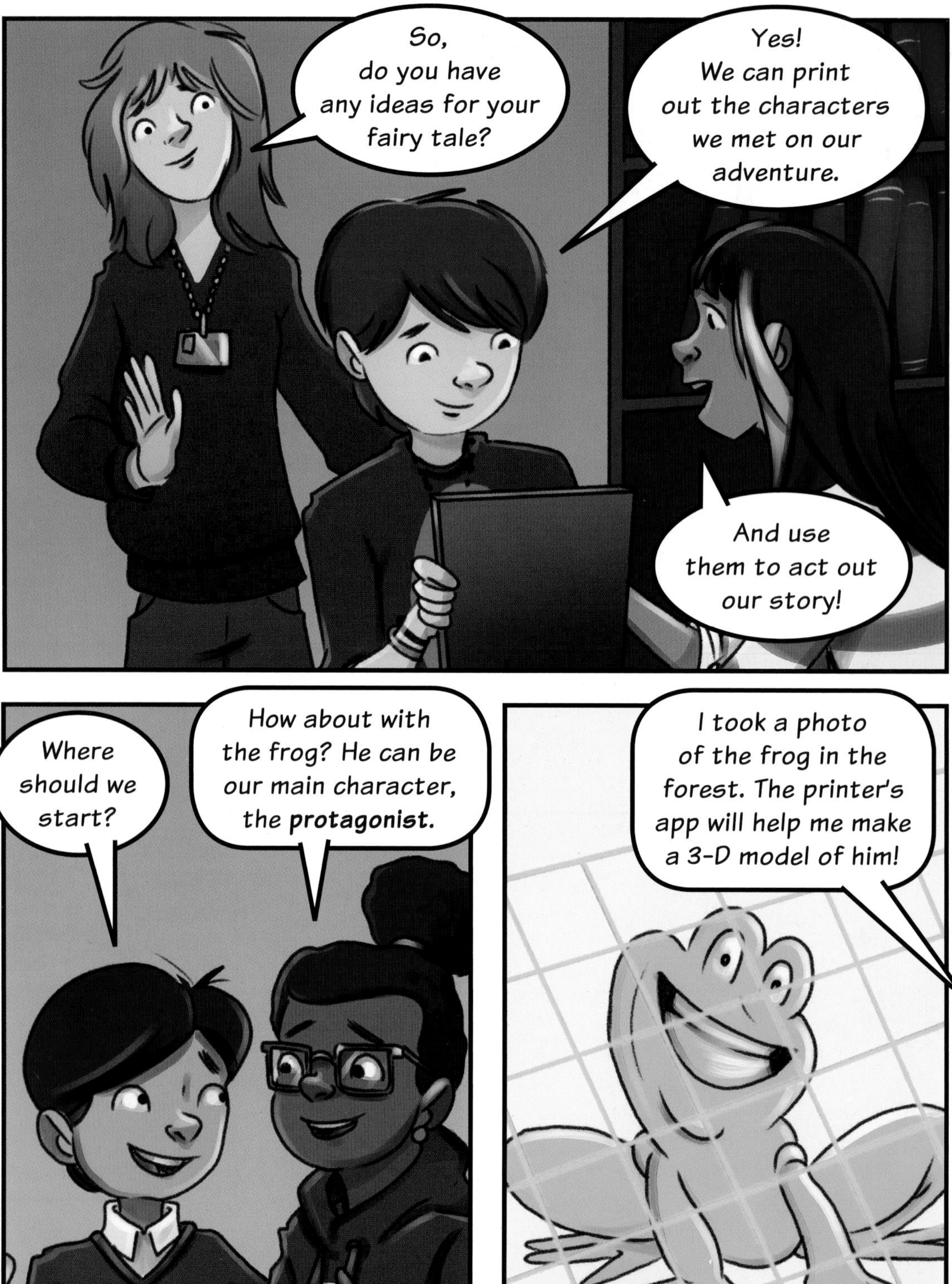
So, do you have any ideas for your fairy tale?
Yes! We can print out the characters we met on our adventure.
And use them to act out our story!
Where should we start?
How about with the frog? He can be our main character, the **protagonist**.
I took a photo of the frog in the forest. The printer's app will help me make a 3-D model of him!

I'm almost done. Eliza, could you put the green filament into the printer?

First, the 3-D printer pulls in the plastic filament and melts the material to a liquid.

Then, the printer squirts a layer of the liquid onto the printing plate. The liquid instantly cools and hardens.

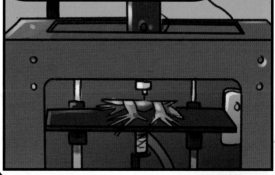

The printer builds one layer at a time until the model is fully formed.

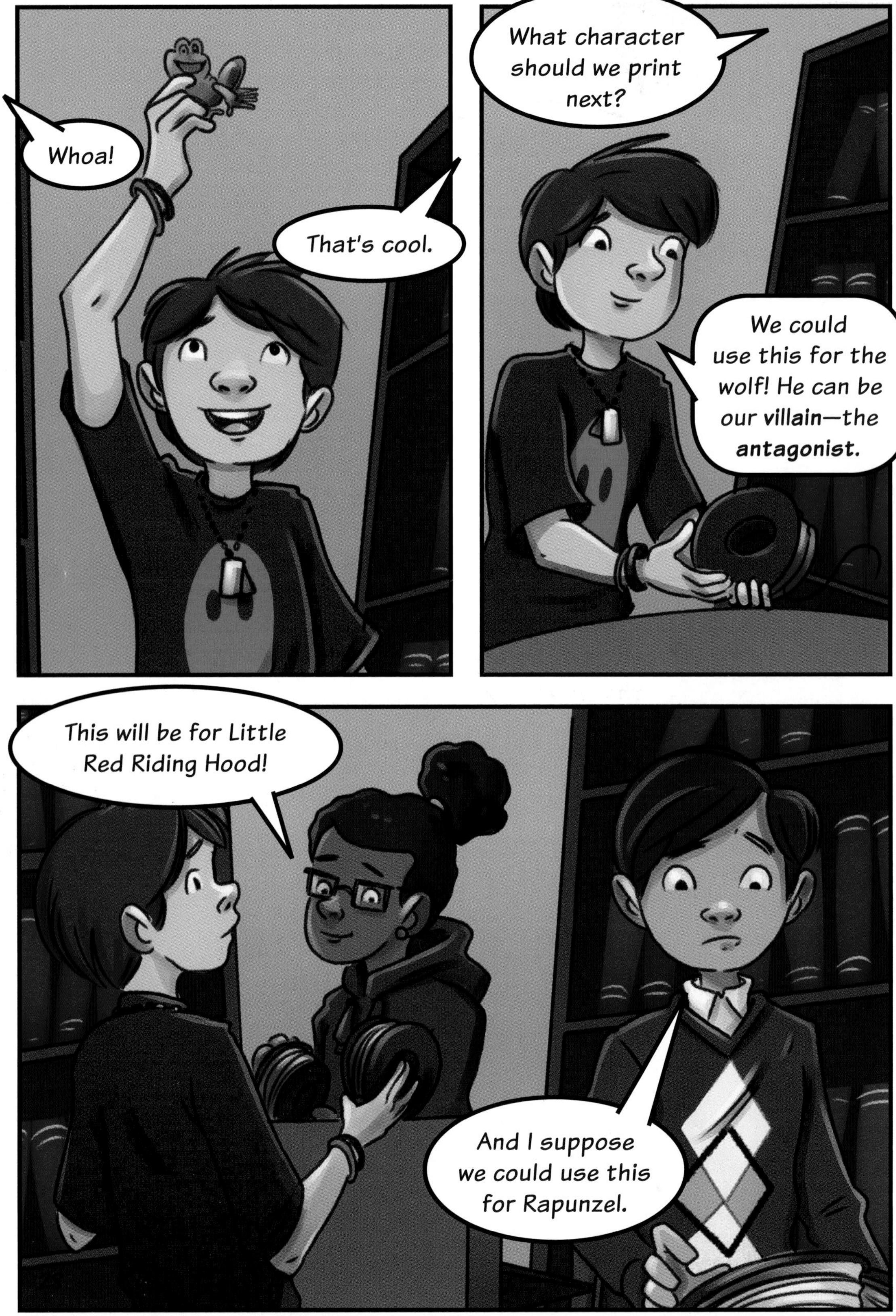
Whoa!
That's cool.
What character should we print next?
We could use this for the wolf! He can be our **villain**—the **antagonist**.
This will be for Little Red Riding Hood!
And I suppose we could use this for Rapunzel.

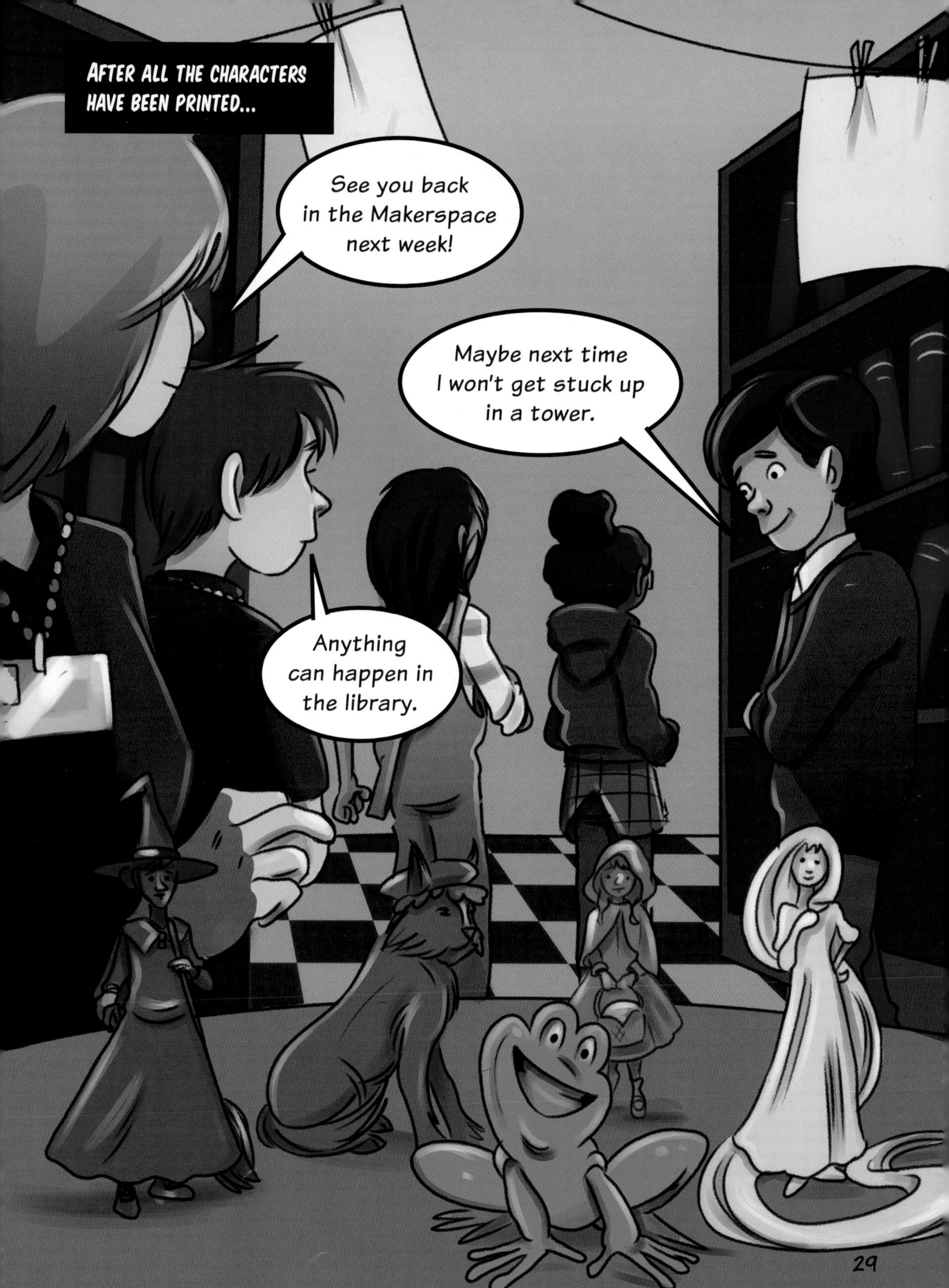
AFTER ALL THE CHARACTERS HAVE BEEN PRINTED...
See you back in the Makerspace next week!
Maybe next time I won't get stuck up in a tower.
Anything can happen in the library.

GLOSSARY

antagonist—person or character that opposes the hero of a story

fairy tale—made-up story, often about magical creatures

filament—thin, flexible thread of material

inductive—relating to the process of using a set of observations to come to a conclusion

logic—system of thinking through problems, often by showing how facts are related

protagonist—leading character or hero of a story

villain—person or character that is evil or opposes the hero of a story

CREATE YOUR OWN MAKERSPACE!

1. Find a place to store supplies. It could be a large area, like the space in this story. But it can also be a cart, bookshelf, or storage bin.

2. Make a list of supplies that you would like to have. Include items found in your recycling bin, such as cardboard boxes, tin cans, and plastic bottles (caps too!). Add art materials, household items such as rubber bands, paper clips, straws, and any other materials useful for planning, building, and creating.

3. Pass out your list to friends and parents. Ask them for help in gathering the materials.

4. It's time to create. Let your imagination run wild!

CREATE YOUR OWN STORY!

Even if you do not have a 3-D printer in your school, you can still make your own characters. You can mold them out of modeling clay or draw them on paper. Once you have characters, you can create your own story!

YOU CAN THINK OF A STORY AS A SIMPLE EQUATION:

PROTAGONIST + PROTAGONIST'S GOAL + ANTAGONIST = STORY

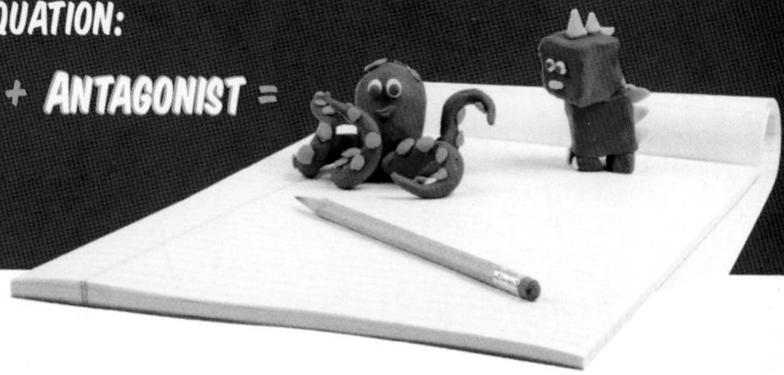

1. **CREATE YOUR PROTAGONIST, OR HERO.** Your protagonist can be anything you imagine: a person, an animal, or even a dancing pineapple! Think of the things this character likes, how the character acts, and whether this character has any special abilities. Then give your protagonist a name.
2. **GIVE YOUR PROTAGONIST A GOAL.** In every story, each character has a goal. It can be anything from finding a hidden treasure to defeating a villain to saving the world.
3. **CREATE AN ANTAGONIST, OR VILLAIN.** An antagonist is anyone or anything that tries to stop your protagonist from reaching a goal. Think of the things this character likes, how the character acts, and whether this character has any special abilities. Then give your antagonist a name.
4. **START WRITING YOUR STORY!** How does your protagonist set out to achieve the goal you described? When the antagonist gets in the way, what happens? How does your protagonist finally achieve the goal?

FURTHER RESOURCES

Hinton, Kerry. *Fab Lab Creating with 3D Scanners.*
New York: Rosen, 2017.

Miller, Shannon McClintock, and Blake Hoena.
A Low-Tech Mission. North Mankato, MN:
Capstone, 2019.

Oakes, Quenton. *Looking Inside a 3D Printer.*
Ann Arbor, MI: Cherry Lake, 2017.

Rackham, Arthur, ill. *Brothers Grimm Fairy Tales:
An Illustrated Classic.* San Diego, CA:
Canterbury Classics, 2017.